Hooked

Club Decadence, Book 7

By

Maddie Taylor

D1523875

Hooked, Club Decadence, Book 7

Published by Maddie Taylor/Breathless Romance

www.RomanceByMaddieTaylor.com

Cover Design by Fantasia Frog Designs

Images by DepositPhotos.com

Editing by Decadent Publishing

Follow Maddie Online

Scan the QR code for all Maddie's Links

<u>Get a FREE Maddie Taylor Romance!</u>
Keep up with author news, get new release updates and cover reveals before anyone else, as well as sneak previews, and lots of giveaways.
Subscribe to Maddie's newsletter ⇨ scan <u>the QR code for the subscribe link</u>

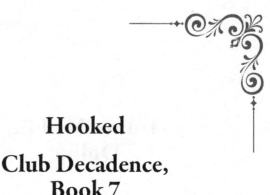

Hooked

Club Decadence, Book 7

AFTER YEARS OF SEARCHING for the dom of her dreams, legal secretary Olivia Wright has all but given up on finding him. With a past full of heartbreak and intermittent dry spells, she is nearly resigned to the life of loneliness that seems to be her fate. She can't even garner the attention of her incredibly handsome boss, although she's certainly tried. Spending eight hours a day in her tightest skirts hasn't tempted the hotshot attorney at all. If anything, it has discouraged Olivia enough to try and move on. When she procures an invitation to Club Decadence, the most exclusive kink club in the state, it seems her luck might finally be changing.

Dapper, dynamic, and disciplined, Joseph Hooks is not your average attorney. He's shamelessly smart, effortlessly powerful, and a stickler for following the rules. Intimidating his opponents in the courtroom comes as naturally as wielding his authority over the submissives he's drawn to in his private life. Although no matter who he's dominating, he never loses control. Until he spots his strictly vanilla secretary taking part in a new member recruitment event at his club. It's hard enough for

Joseph to ignore Olivia and her divine derriere at work; watching her with another dom would be impossible to bear.

Despite his attempts to exercise caution, work and play finally collide. The mutual desire smoldering between him and Olivia for three long years must finally be dealt with. Giving in to temptation will change everything, but Joseph is hopelessly enamored. When he claims her, no matter the obstacles they must hurdle, he's not letting her off his hook.

Publisher's Note: *Hooked* was previously Book 1 of Decadence Nights, a spinoff to the original series. It has been incorporated into Club Decadence as the series continues. It has been revised, reedited, and recovered. All the books in the series are steamy, suspense-filled romances that contain power exchange, BDSM themes, and scenes with graphic violence, which may be disturbing to some.

Chapter 1

THE IMPATIENT DRUMMING of her nails on her desk had synced with the annoyingly loud ticking of the clock on the wall behind her. She shouldn't have been able to hear anything over the sound of the laser printer. But Olivia's attention had zoned in on the minute hand, which seemed to have slowed to a snail's pace the closer it got to quitting time.

While she waited for the last sheet of address labels, she tried to shift focus to something else, in case a clock was like a watched pot. A thud from the next office diverted her attention. Immediately, her mind conjured an image of the man behind the closed door.

At first glance, his classic crew cut, wire-rimmed glasses, and conservative suits—the staple being tweed, which he accessorized with an occasional bow tie—screamed nerd. If he added a pocket protector, he'd fit right in with the tax attorneys and accountants in the suite upstairs. Yet, one only had to be in his presence for a few minutes to learn how wrong first impressions could be.

His six-foot-seven-inch frame instantly turned heads whenever he walked into a room. The sparkle in his gorgeous green eyes, hidden behind the lenses of his round Harry Potter-esque frames, hinted at his quick wit and what she always suspected was a deeply buried mischievous nature. His voice didn't boom like one would expect from a man his size. Instead, its smooth, hypnotic baritone captivated from the first word to the last compelling inflection.

After three years of working at the prestigious Austin law firm, sitting only a few feet from his door and soaking up the authority and understated yet still potent masculinity he exuded, she was in love and lust with Joseph R. Hooks III.

It was unfortunate she'd fallen so hard for him because even though he starred in every one of her naughty daydreams and nighttime fantasies, it couldn't ever be more than that. The firm had a strict no-fraternization policy, and Joseph was nothing if not a stickler for the rules. He was also her boss, but those were the least of the barriers to being with him. Foremost was that in the thirty-seven months, twenty-three days, and seven and a half hours—but who was counting—since she started working as his legal secretary, he had never looked at her with more than a professional interest.

"Ms. Wright." His unusually stern voice pierced the silence of her office.

She swiveled in her chair to find him in front of her desk, frowning down at her.

"Is something wrong, sir?"

"Most assuredly. Stand up, please."

Livia slowly came to her feet. Almost six feet tall in her four-inch heels, she wasn't used to being towered over, but being next to him was like she'd stepped into a hole. Rather than feeling intimidated, the disparity in size made her feel petite and feminine and stirred a primal desire within her to yield to his authority.

"Hands on your desk and assume the position."

The order and his expectations were clear—and shocking.

She gasped in alarm. "You're not serious."

"Ah, but I am. Your actions are a reflection on me. We'll address your recent decline in efficiency here and now, which hopefully will nip it in the bud."

"What did I do?"

"If you give it due consideration, I believe it will come to you."

Calm and collected, her employer rarely got riled, but he didn't tolerate subpar performance and never hesitated to address it, except he'd never done it like this.

He crossed his arms and gazed at her soberly from his lofty height. A glint of something she couldn't quite name, maybe eagerness or arousal—please, let it be arousal—reflected in his beautiful eyes.

"Bend over your desk, Olivia. Procrastination will only earn you more."

Warmth and wetness flooded the needy and long-neglected place between her thighs, dampening her panties. Punishment at Joseph's hand was the best fringe benefit of her job. She'd eagerly give them all up—vacation time, expense account, health, vision, and dental—for this perk alone. As a submissive, she craved his dominance and yearned to be under his control. She also wanted to please him and readily accepted the consequences when she did not.

Rolling her chair out of the way, Livia lowered her upper body from belly to cheek onto the flat surface.

"Skirt up, panties down, little one. You've worked for me long enough to know my requirements."

Little one. Said in his deep, resonant voice, the endearment had her juices flowing, quite literally.

"Yes, sir," she replied, breathless with excitement.

She placed her hands on the desktop to push herself up and bare her bottom as he demanded, but he stopped.

"Maintain your position. You should be able to do as I've ordered from where you are."

Her cheeks flushed hotly. The indignity of being punished by her employer wasn't something she'd soon forget. But presenting her bare bottom by adjusting her own clothing made it seem as though she was a willing accomplice.

And aren't you?

Refusing to answer her own pointed question, she reached back with both hands and tugged her pencil skirt up her thighs. It was no easy task. The snugness increased as the material bunched up, the path becoming more difficult as it traversed her curvy hips and rounded behind. Once she had it high around her waist, she paused.

She'd worn sheer hose and a garter belt. Did he want those down, too? She was about to ask when he beat her to the punch.

"The stockings and garters may stay. They look lovely against your creamy skin, but the panties must go. Pull them down to mid-thigh and keep them there."

As she tugged down her lace and mesh, high-rise bikini briefs, the gusset got caught between her thighs. She had to wiggle and spread her legs to release them. Mortified, Livia bit her bottom lip to contain a moan. What a lewd and jiggly sight that must have been.

As she shifted, cool air brushed against her wet pussy and inner thighs. She wondered if he noticed how aroused she was. Could he see the evidence of her desire on the soaked satin or smell her lustful scent?

"Good girl," he murmured, stepping closer.

She managed to suppress a groan at his praise, but her control was further tested when his warm hand ran over her bottom cheeks. She failed as a shudder swept through her needy body.

He did not mention her reaction. Instead, he continued with his instructions. "I expect you to behave while receiving your punishment as well. No blocking or squirming, and no name-calling directed at me or any of my ancestors. You will hold your position for the count of one hundred."

"One hundred!" she exclaimed in dismay.

"I pay you well for precision and won't tolerate sloppiness or mistakes." His large hand glided over her taut globes and down to her thighs, his fingertips wandering dangerously close to her center. He'd find her wet, which would increase her mortification. She had a brief reprieve when he announced, "We'll begin with a hand spanking."

But the implication there would be more soon had her imagination running wild. What would follow? A paddle? His belt? Or one of the rattan canes he kept in an umbrella stand in the corner of his office.

As she pondered the course of her punishment, from the corner of her eye, she saw him draw back his broad hand. Alongside her dread, a thrill of excitement rushed through her, channeling more liquid heat to her pussy.

Dear heaven! She was a grown woman, a professional. Did she actually want him to punish her like a willful child?

Although her rational mind shouted, *no!* her highly aroused body screamed, *Hell, yes!* Having him touch her in every way possible was her dream come true.

Her breath froze in her chest as she waited with carnal anticipation for his hand to land the first solid spank.

Screech! Clack, clack. Crunch!

The harsh, grating noises made her jump, which jarred her from her daydream. So lost in her erotic fantasy, the sudden movement sent her off-balance, and she almost fell off her chair. Once she steadied herself, her head snapped around to identify the source. No big shock. It was her printer and another damn paper jam.

"Just when I was getting to the best part, too," Livia grumbled.

She'd given up on the recurring fantasy ever becoming a reality for many reasons. Joseph was a consummate professional and had never been what she would call stern with her, nor did he find fault in her work. She never gave him a reason to.

Livia took pride in her work and paid meticulous attention to detail. Everything she presented to her boss, whether court documents, discovery binders, his transcribed notes, or something as simple as an interoffice memo, was tidy and precise, like her desk and attire. Furthermore, he had an umbrella in the stand in his office, not whippy canes for disciplining his staff.

She drew a deep breath while covertly rubbing her hard nipples with her forearms. Looking down, there they were, clearly visible through her lace bra and silk blouse. Anyone she crossed paths with would notice.

Forcing herself to focus on her work, she turned to battle her nemesis: the hated all-in-one wireless printer.

After ten minutes of picking out bits of paper and resetting the infernal machine, cursing it the whole while under her breath, a page of labels shot out into the tray. She speedily affixed the stickers to the remaining envelopes.

With her last task of the day completed, Livia glanced at the wall clock again and did some quick calculations. She would be home in twenty minutes. With an hour to shower, do her hair and makeup, and another two hours for the drive from Austin, she would arrive at the club by eight thirty.

"Plenty of time," she murmured as she slid the weighed and stamped envelopes into the outgoing tray.

She tidied up, putting away the envelopes and extra labels then logged out of her computer. "Only one more thing to do, and I'm out of here."

Livia reached for her desk phone and depressed the intercom button, frowning upon noticing a chip in her newly polished nails. The gel manicure she had gotten last night was supposed to last weeks, not hours.

Faintly, she heard the buzz in the next office.

A moment later, a deep voice answered, "Yes, Olivia?"

"I'm leaving for the day, sir."

There was a pause. "It's not quite 4:30."

Startled, she stared at her phone. They'd discussed this only yesterday, although she shouldn't be surprised. He often lost track of what was happening in the world while preparing for a big case.

During these times, he reminded her of the absent-minded professor, but he was actually a brilliant trial attorney. The

Austin legal community called him the lethal litigator due to the many high-profile capital murder defendants he'd represented. She believed it had a lot to do with his tough-as-nails reputation and a near-perfect acquittal record as well. In fact, during her tenure with him, he hadn't lost a single case. To truly appreciate how he'd earned it required a trip to court to see him in action or a brief chat with the opposing counsel after he eviscerated them.

But he wasn't the stereotypical rich, arrogant, amoral asshole. They were out there; Lord knows she'd worked for a few, and TV dramas portrayed them that way for a reason.

Yes, he drove a Jag—sleek, black, and pretentious—and he lived in an enormous house on Lake Travis in Costa Bella, a gated community about twenty minutes northwest of the city. He also did a notable amount of pro bono work, was invested in programs that served underprivileged youth, and served on three advisory boards for charities that focused on childhood education, community outreach, and women's health.

He didn't speak of his personal life, but his degree on the wall was from UT right there in Austin. Through the office rumor mill, she'd learned his mother was a nurse, but no one had ever met his father. It explained a lot, including why he didn't get his JD from one of the prestigious Ivy League Law schools back East. Maybe hard work and humble beginnings factored into his success and was why he seemed more grounded than some of the obnoxious Harvard-educated jerks she'd worked for previously.

Not that Joseph couldn't be aggressive and argumentative or a persnickety pain in the ass, particularly with her and the junior associates assigned to him. He was also single-minded and laser-focused when going to trial, but those were the traits of a good litigator. And he was that way because his client's future, and whether they walked free or faced a lifetime confined behind steel bars, depended on him being at the top of his game.

But he possessed a softer side. She'd seen it in his generosity to his causes and with his employees. And she'd heard his joy for life in his rich laughter. Although it didn't come often, it stirred a warmth inside her that wasn't appropriate in a law office. He had a sharp wit, a dry sense of humor, and could be utterly charming. If not, she wouldn't be so smitten with him.

"You have plans."

His voice coming from the doorway behind her instead of through the speaker had Livia spinning in her chair. Having discarded his jacket, he stood in shirtsleeves, his tie still knotted impeccably at his throat. Her gaze drifted upward beyond the dotted navy-blue silk to his darkened jaw, which bore a healthy scruff of five-o'clock shadow. What would it feel like against her neck if he kissed there? Better yet, on her inner thighs with his mouth on her—

"Olivia?"

She blinked, her fantasy replaced by his handsome face. Realizing he expected a response, she replied haltingly, her heart racing, a common reaction to his presence. "Yes. I, uh...have an...engagement this evening."

"An engagement," he repeated as his brows drew together, forming three small vertical lines between them.

"Yes, sir. I took an abbreviated lunch so I could leave early today."

Despite her lustful thoughts about the man standing tall and delicious only a few feet away, her tone remained even, which was the hallmark of her imperturbable professionalism, her patience being legendary among the legal secretaries in the six-partner group.

After years with the firm, working for their top criminal defense attorney, who was reputed to be the most demanding taskmaster of the bunch, she was used to his penchant for timeliness.

"I mentioned this to you on Monday, remember?"

After another brief pause, where he considered her closely, he nodded. "It slipped my mind, but I recall now. Are you traveling?" He glanced at the window. "The forecast is for severe storms and heavy rain this evening."

Turning, she followed his gaze to her window, seeing nothing but sunshine beaming in. "I have about an hour's drive."

"Unless it is urgent, the weather service advises everyone to stay close to home tonight. Besides, I worry about you in that car—"

"I just had it in the shop for a tune-up, sir. I'm sure I'll be fine."

The frown lines deepened then his lips parted on an indrawn breath, making Livia believe he would object further. Instead, he suddenly let it go, whatever it was.

"Run along, then, Olivia, but use extreme caution on the roads tonight. I'd like to have you here in one piece tomorrow."

"I'll be cautious, sir. Thank you."

Thinking she'd been dismissed, she moved to the credenza against the far wall and bent to retrieve her purse from the bottom drawer. When she stood and turned, he had moved a few steps farther into her office. He stood closer now, his pensive gaze aimed downward. If she didn't know better, she would have said he was checking out her upturned bottom. She laughed in her head, scolding herself for hopelessly pining for something that would never come true.

He said nothing further, though he didn't leave. Livia inhaled, about to ask if something was wrong, but she caught a hint of his cologne, Ralph Lauren's Red Polo. She'd recognize it anywhere. Her favorite male scent—probably because Joseph wore it. At the mall, she often went by the men's counter at Dillard's for a sample card, even if it was out of the way. Then, like a lovesick fool, she'd wander through the stores, sniffing it and thinking of him.

Her phone alarm went off, a welcome diversion from her very distracting boss. "I should go, or I'll be late. Was there anything else?"

Wordlessly, he scanned her face. Livia returned his scrutiny, noting that in the afternoon sun filtering in through her window, they appeared nearly blue, which was a change from their usual brilliant green. Over the years, she noticed they changed subtly with the color of his shirt or tie but more so with extreme emotions, which he rarely revealed. She'd seen them a greenish-brown when he focused on a tough defense, and once, when angry, they'd turned a deep forest green. Like the man himself, his eyes were enigmatic.

She always wondered how they would appear at the height of passion.

Realizing she was staring, she averted her gaze and tried to collect herself. But he suddenly cleared his throat, shifting as though uncomfortable, which was unlike the confident man she knew then strode back inside his office.

She heard him say, "Have a pleasant night, Olivia," before the latch on the door clicked softly behind him.

With him out of sight, she didn't have to quell the tremor of excitement that ran through her. He'd shown concern for her safety, but that wasn't unusual. He'd always been considerate, holding the door for her or helping her with her coat. If they went out to meet with clients or for depositions, he walked beside her with a guiding hand on the small of her back or beneath her elbow.

That was as far as it went, much to her regret.

He was a gentleman and a throwback to a courtlier time. His mannerly ways were part of his appeal. So rarely did men hold a chair or open a car door for their dates anymore. Women's strides for independence had backfired on the social niceties they once enjoyed, which Livia, who was rather old-fashioned, sorely missed.

He also had an air of authority, which in other men she found off-putting, but from Joseph, it was different, more of an innate sense of confidence. He ruled his domain with a quiet authority rather than an iron fist, which she also found very attractive.

Before her, rumor had it he'd gone through secretaries like water through a sieve. Some girls still with the firm accused him of having a stick up his ass, although not to his face. Livia realized how his demand for order and exactness might be viewed as perfectionism and, as a boss, make him hard to get along with, if not impossible, to please. She was okay with it, though, preferring knowing what to expect rather than the other partners' chaos and unpredictability.

Having survived three years in his employ, she was the longest in the position in his twelve-year tenure with the firm. Sadly, in all that time, he'd never shown the slightest interest in her other than as a valued employee. Self-consciously smoothing down her skirt, she asked herself, for the millionth time, why.

Was she too tall, too short, too soft and curvy? Was it her perfume or that he didn't like blondes? She'd often wondered if it was her clothing. She went with a conservative style at the office but not dowdy. It was Ann Taylor after all. Consignment shop Ann Taylor because of her meager budget, meaning it was a few years behind current fashion, but it was her usual pencil skirt and blouse. Did those ever go out of style?

It was also snug enough on her five-foot-seven, one hundred fifty-pound frame to show off her curves, which she had plenty of, but not be tastelessly tight. Today, she'd topped the winter-white skirt with a floral shell in blues and corals, a coral jacket, and matching heels—double strap, four-inch heels—which were playful but not over the top for work.

She'd been in and out of his office a dozen times today, but he never seemed to notice, unlike the other partners who she often caught staring at her legs or her ass, and most especially her D-cup breasts. She often rationalized that he might prefer men, but that was sour grapes on her part because he never lacked female company.

As the saying went, he just wasn't into her. Still, what had his odd look just now been about?

She pushed away the silly notion, admonishing herself silently for seeing something that wasn't there. For years she'd subtly flirted, hinting and hoping, but walked away disappoint-

ed time and again. She'd finally given up, conceding it was unlikely he'd ever return her feelings, that her love was unrequited
and further efforts were futile. At least that's what her rational
mind said, but she had no control over her irrational heart and
ungovernable libido.

With a deep, disappointed sigh, she switched off her desk
lamp. He clearly didn't see her as more than a loyal employee.
She smiled to herself. If he saw her in the outfit she planned to
wear at the club tonight, maybe she'd earn a second glance.

As she walked to the door, the painting on the wall across
from her desk caught her eye. It was a reproduction of Bier-
stadt's Emerald Sea. In it, the blues and greens of a turbulent
sea contrasted with the blues and grays of a stormy sky. As she
stared at the choppy white caps, she realized they weren't so
much emerald as aquamarine, the same color as Joseph's eyes,
before he abruptly vanished inside his office. Although she'd
looked at the print every day, five days a week, fifty-two weeks a
year, and noted the beautiful blue-green hue, she'd never seen it
on him and had to wonder what crossed his mind that caused
the sudden change.

Chapter 2

OLIVIA DIDN'T MAKE it out the door, stopped again by a familiar voice. "Hey, girl! Tonight's the big night. You ready to get your spank on?"

Horrified, she glanced at the office door. Seeing it still closed—thank goodness—she rushed out to meet her friend Emma before she said something else outrageous.

Livia motioned for her to be quiet. "Shh. Keep your voice down. Someone will hear you."

"Someone like your bow-tie-wearing, tall drink of water, you mean?" she asked with a grin.

"He isn't mine, but yes, he might, and anyone else who's around. I'd rather not have my social calendar become fodder for the firm's gossip mill, if you don't mind."

"What social calendar? The last time you went out, other than with David and me, was six months ago."

"That's no one's business, either," she hissed, speaking low and hoping her friend would follow suit.

"Chill, hon. No one's going to hear. It's ten after five. Anyone still around at closing time hauled ass out of here nine minutes and fifty-nine seconds ago."

"Oh no. Is it that late?" Livia pulled out her phone to check. Sure enough. 5:11. The batteries in the wall clock must need changing. Either that or her daydreams about Joseph had sucked up more time than she thought. "I have to get a move on, or the club will be closed by the time I make it to San Antonio."

"Decadence is a sex club, babe. I'm pretty sure they stay open past nine."

She frantically surveyed the area for who may have heard before giving her best friend an irritated glance. "Will you please stop!"

"Sorry," she replied, her grin saying she wasn't sorry in the least. Emma looped her arm through hers. "Come on. I'll walk out with you."

Emma was married to David Briscoe, a dear friend she'd met while in college. They had grown close because they had so much in common, and now she was her best friend. A paralegal at the firm for years, she'd told her when a secretarial position had opened up. She'd also put in a good word for her with the manager in HR. Despite her glowing recommendation, Livia had to sit through three nerve-racking interviews, the last one with Joseph, who had the final say on who became his legal secretary, of course.

Emma was the only person she could confide in about the lustful feelings she had for her boss. They were close, like sisters, and like an older sister, she didn't let an opportunity to tease her about it pass by.

"Maybe it wouldn't hurt for Joe to know you're in the market for a dom. It might open his eyes to the smoking-hot submissive parked outside his door who has been going unnoticed, un-spanked, and un-fucked for too damn long. Then, if he still doesn't get his head out of his ass and stake his claim, you can finally move on."

"Emma Jean Briscoe, if you dare utter a single word to him, you'll have to find a new best friend because I will be on my way to Vancouver, having packed my belongings and skulked out of town in the wee hours, never to be seen at this firm again. Is that what you want?"

"You don't mean that. And may I point out, you're making more noise than I did."

"I'm dead serious. Besides, you said the S-word. That tends to get folk's attention pretty darn quick."

"Submissive?"

"Shh!" Grabbing her arm, she pulled her down the hall, through the lobby, past the empty reception desk, and out the front door. On the sidewalk out front, with the traffic noise giving the relative privacy, Livia set her straight. "Not S as in sub. S as in spanked."

"Ah." Emma's pretty blue eyes sparkled with humor. "You've got a point there. A good old-fashioned hiding, especially in Texas, makes people stand up and take notice. Or should I say bend over?"

"I don't have time for your nonsense today," she muttered as she took off down the sidewalk to the employee parking lot.

Still laughing at her own joke, Emma hurried after her. When her much shorter legs caught up, she was out of breath. "Why not let David and me take you to the Pit tomorrow night? We can be your wingmen and help you scope out a nice local dom."

She shot a frowning glance at her friend. "Sorry, but a club called the Pleasure Pit doesn't exactly inspire confidence. Besides, you said that place was a meat market full of posers and wannabes."

She blinked as if she didn't recall. "I did?"

"Yes, you called it that several times, as a matter of fact."

"Mm," Em grunted. "I guess I did. We haven't been in a while."

Tilting her head, Livia's brows arched as she challenged, "And why is that?"

A blush crept into her friend's cheeks as she sheepishly admitted, "Because it's a meat market full of posers and wannabes."

"I rest my case." Having arrived at her car, she plunked her purse down on the hood and went fishing for her car keys.

"It might be different now," Emma said then went on, her voice filled with concern, "I worry about you going to a club you've never been to before, by yourself, two hours from home."

Livia stopped digging and glanced her way. "I know you have reservations, but I'm a big girl. I promise if don't feel comfortable, I'll leave." She reached for Em's hand and gave it a squeeze. "You both said this is the best club in the Southwest and I don't think David would have gone to the trouble of getting me this invitation if he didn't think I'd be safe."

"He arranged for an escort," she reminded her.

"Even better. I'll have a friend of a friend looking out for me."

"I'm afraid it might be more than you can handle. From what I hear, this club is the real deal. The owners are ex-Special Forces—Green Berets—who don't take shit from anyone, especially their subs."

"And your point is?"

"Liv..."

"I'm not stupid, Em. Nor am I inexperienced, just a tad rusty."

"That's what I'm saying. You haven't had a dom since Vaughn. How long has that been? Three years?"

"So?"

She didn't want to think about Vaughn, not tonight or ever.

After two years with the rat bastard, out of the blue, he ended it. She'd been crushed, especially when she saw him less than a month later with her replacement on his arm. A petite blonde with blatantly obvious fake boobs, an extremely short skirt, and younger than her by a decade, at least. What stung worse than being replaced by a twenty-something was the collar around her neck, something Vaughn hadn't given her until she "proved herself" six months in.

"Since you're out of practice, maybe you should ease back into the game. Let me fix you up with Evan, David's friend."

"He's a kid."

"He's thirty."

"Compared to me, that's a kid. He's also inexperienced. You said David only started mentoring him last month. No thanks."

"He's a good-natured, sweet guy."

"That's just it. I don't want good-natured and sweet. I want a badass Green Beret who oozes masculinity and dominance from his pores."

"Don't we all," Emma muttered. "I think you've been reading too many BDSM romances because that's not realistic. Especially if you expect to scoop up an owner. I heard the last one just recently went off the market."

"You hear a lot about a club that's supposedly ultra-exclusive where you're not a member."

"We're not members because the annual fees are astronomical," she admitted. "Please, reconsider Evan. David said he's taking to it like a fish to water."

Livia frowned at her well-meaning but persistent friend. "Is David good-natured and sweet?"

After a moment's consideration, she replied with a hesitant, "Well...yeah... He's sweet in his own good-natured kind of way."

"You are so full of it. Or was it a different Emma who called me last weekend to cancel our shopping trip because you were having trouble walking?"

"A man can be well-endowed, high-octane between the sheets, and still be sweet."

"True, but that wasn't the problem, as I recall. He was trying to work, but you wouldn't stop pestering him. According to your detailed play-by-play"—here she stopped and glanced around to make sure no one would hear—"he gagged you, tied you to the bed, plugged your ass, and attached or inserted battery-powered vibrating devices to your other parts while he finished his work in peace."

"See what I mean," she said with a sigh. "That was sweet."

Livia rolled her eyes and then drove her point home. "Does he get your heart pumping with only a look? Does the tone of his voice when he goes alpha on your naughty ass make you tremble with excitement? When he tells you in no uncertain terms what to do in the bedroom, does he make your panties wet? If he lets you wear any, that is."

"Liv!" Emma gasped, her face flaming scarlet.

"See? You have that. Why can't I?" By verbalizing her own fantasies, she'd made herself even more determined to go. She resumed digging for her keys.

"You'll find him, hon."

She didn't glance up, still searching. "I'm really starting to doubt that, and my clock is ticking."

"Wait!"

Emma grabbed her arm just as she snagged her keys. When she jerked, spinning her a quarter turn to face her, they slipped from her grasp. Livia silently groaned, knowing they'd sink into the abyss of her purse where she couldn't find them again. At this rate, she'd be in San Antonio by midnight if she was lucky.

"Did you just say you wanted a baby? Since when? Is that what this is about?"

Livia rolled her eyes. "Not that clock. My countdown to forty." While she explained, she laid her wallet and all the other stuff from her purse on the hood of her car to make her search easier. "Once I hit the big 4-0, my odds of finding a husband and getting that white picket fence are a pathetic 2.6 percent. My pool of candidates is dwindling as we speak."

She didn't want a baby. She wanted two, a boy and a girl, a husband, the house in suburbia, a dog, and yes, the proverbial white picket fence. And when she married, she also wanted her husband to be her dom. Was that too much to ask?

At your age, probably.

The unfortunate truth rattled around in her brain, as it always did when she went down this path. She'd done the research and the math on this extensively. Statistically speaking, if she reached forty without finding her man, her chances were a dismal slim to none.

"Only 2.6 percent, Em," she repeated in a whisper. "Can you believe that?"

Her friend wrapped her arm around her waist in a side hug and squeezed her tight. "Don't give up hope, honey. You're a yummy snack and a half. Besides, what do statisticians know about love and romance?"

"Numbers don't lie. Eliminating all the vanilla men reduces my already minuscule odds of finding Mr. Right by another two-thirds. And that's being generous, considering only a third of that pool has only fantasized about BDSM but never actually took part in it. Since I want someone experienced, it's more like a tenth, which makes my odds of finding a good dom, marrying, and having the family I want before my eggs turn to dust much, much worse. Less than half of one percent by my calculations, which is pathetic."

After her long-winded speech, she leaned on her Toyota and dropped her head on the hood in defeat. There were tears in her eyes when she looked at her friend a moment later.

"How the hell am I supposed to find Master Less-Than-One-In-A-Hundred, Em? And if I do, how do I know he won't turn out to be another Vaughn Steros?"

"Oh, honey."

"Maybe I should forget about love altogether and get a cat—or ten."

"You're upset. Don't go to San Antonio tonight. Come have dinner with David and me instead."

Sorely tempted, Livia actually considered ditching her plans. But if she didn't go, she'd always wonder what might have been. Perhaps tonight was the night she was supposed to meet the dom of her dreams. Joseph's handsome face appeared in her mind's eye as if to remind her that her dream dom for the past few years was him.

But wishes and dreams, were just that, and for her rarely came true.

"I'm going," she said determinedly. "And now I have to really hurry because I have a million things to do." She held up her finger with the damaged nail. "Correction, a million and one."

"Olivia Wright," Emma exclaimed with her hands on her hips. "Flipping me off is uncalled for. I'm just trying to help."

Despite her blue mood, she laughed. "Inadvertent bird, Em. Sorry," she said, hitting the auto locks on the key fob she finally located. "I have to add nail repair to my long list of things to do before I hit the road."

After she threw everything back in her bag and climbed behind the wheel, she forced a smile as she looked up at Emma standing beside her door.

"Wish me luck. If I make it by nine, it will be a miracle."

"Be careful," Emma urged as she reached in and squeezed her shoulder. "Both on the road and at the club. You have a safeword, don't forget. And don't take any shit from any of those drill sergeant dominants. You have the real power, not them." She winked when she added, "Unless they're as hot as they say, and you really want them to drill you, that is."

"Emma!" she exclaimed, letting out a little laugh. "You know, I have a feeling about tonight. Something is going to happen. I'm not exactly sure what, but I'll be in a new city, a new club, and with new people. This may be my last shot, so I'm going for it."

"Babe, as gorgeous as you are, you're going to rock their world."

She stepped back to let Livia shut her door. Obviously needing to say more, she tapped on her window. As soon as it unrolled, she started in again.

"Call me for a safety check when you get there and when you're ready to head home."

"Yes, Mom," she replied with a wave then started the ignition.

Despite her bluster with Emma just now, she was a nervous wreck. Her hands trembled visibly when she shifted into reverse. As she pulled out of the lot, she started planning contingencies if things didn't go as planned, like where she would get her new cat—or ten.

Chapter 3

WHEN SHE ARRIVED AT a minute before nine, the line was out the door. A half hour later, she made it into the lobby. When she was the next to register, a man in black entered the lobby and quietly surveyed the scene. Livia had to concentrate on not staring. Under the lights, glints of red shone in his thick brown hair, and he had the most stunning midnight-blue eyes. He moved with fluid grace as he crossed to the door; the muscles of his chest and biceps strained the fabric of his black silk shirt.

"Ladies," he began, addressing the line of women still waiting outside on the steps. His voice, as smooth as the finest Belgian chocolate, silenced their chatter instantly. "Regrettably, we are at capacity."

There were a few grumbles of disappointment but mostly awed silence.

"To make it up to you, I have VIP vouchers for two weeks from now. Arrive by eight, and you have my personal guarantee of admittance, and a table in the lounge near the stage."

A moment later, he stood beside Livia at the high counter. He laid his large hand with its long, broad fingers and carefully manicured nails flat on the gleaming mahogany top as he spoke to the girl checking everyone in.

"Hurry it along if you can, Astrid. I can't hold them off much longer. Elena goes on in five, check-in completed or not."

"Yes, Master Dex," she answered softly, her eyes flicking to the man with unconcealed adoration.

He nodded, spared Livia a brief glance then disappeared inside the double doors behind them.

"Who was that?" she asked Astrid, her mouth gone dry.

"Isn't he gorgeous?" the girl all but cooed. "Sadly, he's taken. The same as all the owners, since Angie corralled Master T. He was the most elusive of the bunch. The irony, which has everyone shocked is that she was vanilla before she met him." As if realizing she had probably shared too much, she rushed to say, "There are plenty more available doms though. Don't you worry."

She took Livia's paperwork, which included of a confidentiality agreement and a mini-questionnaire and scanned it. Then she handed her a pink ribbon from the pile of pink, red, and white ones in front of her. "Wear this somewhere visible, in your hair or around your neck. The wrist is good, too."

"What does it mean?"

"It tells interested tops and doms your experience level."

"Pink signifying what?"

"Intermediate. White is novice and red means an old pro," she giggled. Then her hand flew to her mouth. "Not that kind of pro. I didn't mean—"

"I think she knows what you meant, Astrid," said another man who had appeared out of nowhere. He was just as gorgeous as the last one, and even taller.

"I'm sorry, Master Sean. I can't seem to keep from putting my foot in my mouth."

"I spoke with Master J a few minutes ago. He's on his way but running late. Maybe we can get him to work on those loose lips in the playroom after your shift tonight?"

She blanched but bowed her head dutifully. "If you think that's best, sir."

"Not Master J?"

Although she looked reluctant to, she shook her head and whispered, "He uses a cane."

"Dano is also available—"

"Oh yes," she gushed, her face lighting up with a wistful smile. "Please, sir. A lesson from Master D would be wonderful."

Master Sean shook his head. "Leery of the cane, but not of the sadist. Amazing."

He scribbled something on a piece of paper, folded it, and tucked it into one of her wrist cuffs. "Report to him after you've finished here."

"Yes, sir. Thank you." She beamed up at the man and then turned to collect the last girl's papers.

Master Sean turned to Livia. "The show starts any minute, little sub. Best head on in."

He strode to the door and pushed it open, holding it for her. His gaze shot behind her then returned. "No girl posse for moral support?"

"No, sir, I'm alone. I was supposed to meet someone here, but she had to cancel at the last minute."

David would be furious if he knew she'd gone on by herself, but she didn't plan on him finding out.

"Let me find you a friend," the beautiful Adonis offered.

As they stepped inside, his vibrant blue eyes, not midnight like the other but more of a sky blue and just as compelling, scanned the crowded room. Suddenly, he grinned.

"This way." He was speaking loudly to be heard over the band who had just begun playing and the crowd that was cheering wildly. "What's your name?"

"Olivia, sir."

He wrapped his hand around her wrist and pulled her through the throng of people. It seemed more like a concert than a mixer, as she assumed it would be. At a table up front, he stopped behind a stunning redhead in an off-the-shoulder black dress. He wrapped her long ponytail around his wrist and pulled her head back until she was looking up at him. Livia noticed the huge smile on her face before Master Sean's lips lowered and he devoured her mouth.

After several minutes, he raised his head. "I brought you a guest, nightingale. Olivia, this is my sub Mara." He pulled up a chair and seated Livia beside her. "She'll keep you company until someone claims you."

"She's lovely, master," the green-eyed beauty said, her cheeks flushed and slightly breathless from the passionate kiss. She still managed a friendly smile. "My guess is that won't take very long."

"We've got a room at eleven, baby," Sean murmured privately in her ear, although his voice carried to Livia. "Don't be late or the sultan won't be happy."

"Never. Tardiness would be an insult." She flashed a serene smile. "I'll make sure to bring my seven veils, for the supreme potentate's enjoyment."

He grinned, clearly in love with his submissive, and took her lips again, briefly. "I'm on crowd control, gotta go."

Enthralled by the affection between the two, she watched as Mara followed him with her eyes until he was out of sight.

"How long have you been together?"

"Which time?" she replied, a dreamy quality to her voice as she turned back. She held up her left hand and flashed her wedding rings. "The second time stuck. Well, it was actually still the first. I just didn't know it." Noticing Livia's puzzled expression, she shook her head. "Sorry, long story."

She shouted to be heard over the screaming fans. "Elena's doing a set of her Pink covers. Relax and enjoy. Nothing will happen until she's done. Trust me."

IT TOOK HIM TWENTY minutes to get from the doors to the bar, the crowd standing shoulder to shoulder. There was a party atmosphere in the club tonight, but Joseph wasn't in the mood. He couldn't believe he'd come on a Wednesday, the busiest night of the night second to Saturday. He'd left Austin on a whim, usually only coming to play on weekends. But he felt the need to blow off steam and some long pent-up sexual frustration. It seemed that would have to wait until after Elena's concert.

Irritated, he blew out a breath and veered left to where two of the owners, Rick Spencer and Jonas Mitchell, were sitting, keeping an eye on things from a corner of the bar. Doubtless, a priority was the table near the stage where their submissives always sat. Six in all, seven if you counted the silent partner, Major General Peter Davis, who wasn't quite so silent since retiring from the Army. The owners all came from the same Special Forces detachment. After leaving the service, they had settled in San Antonio, home to most of them, and embarked on two very lucrative ventures, Club Decadence and Rossi Security, Inc.

The Rossi group was high profile, not least of all their pivotal role in shutting down a major drug cartel in South Texas. The club, on the other hand, was private, but word had spread quickly to the kink inclined and BDSM communities from coast to coast of this jewel, nestled in the hills a few miles north of the city.

Joseph was privy to most of the inner workings of the group having represented the owners for several years. Usually not one to delve into contract law, he made an exception because of the sensitive nature of the club's business. He soon found it was only a small fraction of the work he did for the group, case in point, his recent representation of one of their subs for attempted murder charges.

Bumped into from behind by a bouncing cheering young woman, he scowled. With too long of a drive to go home now, he determined to deal with it as best he could—with alcohol. He shouldered his way through the throng with the taste for a bracing shot of scotch on his tongue.

"Joseph," Rick called in greeting. "You look harried."

"Beer?" Jonas asked as he flagged down the bartender.

He shook his head. "Single malt, top shelf."

Jonas grunted. "One of those days, eh? Highland Park 25 for Joseph, Ben."

The bar manager's eyes widened. Jonas had gone beyond the top shelf and ordered him a shot from a $500 bottle of scotch.

"Dex got a case as a thank-you from a client," Rick explained. "Only you and Cap drink the stuff, so it's yours whenever you want it."

"Appreciated." A stool opened beside Jonas, and he sat, taking off his glasses and rubbing his tired eyes. "Elena really pulls in a crowd."

"Yeah, too big," Jonas commented as he shifted to survey the room. "We're going to have to move our open sub night to when Elena isn't headlining. It defeats the purpose when the submissives are hanging around the stage instead of the dominants."

"Good idea," Joseph agreed. "It's almost ten and I haven't had time to circulate, not that I could in this crush."

"Still on the hunt for the perfect sub, old man?" Rick chuckled. "Don't get discouraged, she's out there."

"Let's hope she wasn't among the two dozen or so Dex had to turn away at the door," Sean put in as he came up behind them. "He hates doing that. There were a lot of disappointed faces when he broke the news. He gave them vouchers, hoping they'll return next time. Unfortunately, some won't have the nerve."

"What was the breakdown tonight?" Rick inquired.

"Twelve red, fourteen white," Sean replied.

"No pink?" Jonas asked in surprise.

"Only one. A stunning blonde. She came in alone, so I sat her with the girls."

Jonas whistled. "That's a brave girl."

"More like a brave woman. Mid-thirties, I'm guessing."

"She might be what you're looking for, Joe," suggested Rick. "Not a newbie to try your patience or too well trained not to offer a challenge."

"I think you gentlemen have read my file," Joseph murmured as he pulled out a linen handkerchief and cleaned his lenses.

The three owners chuckled. When he settled his frames back on his nose, he followed their eyes to the head table. Their lovely ladies were instantly recognizable, fixtures in the club for months, some for years. Except Mara, who wasn't actually new but had been absent for a time. His eyes fell on the woman sitting next to her. The long golden fall of wavy blonde hair made him surge to his feet. Even across the jam-packed room, she was achingly familiar.

It can't be.

Sidestepping to get a better look, he was thankful for his above-average height that gave him a better view over the crowd. He watched as her head tilted back, sending the blonde waves brushing across her shoulders and the curled ends bouncing along her back. Almost positive of her identify, all doubt disappeared when his body responded to her as it had so often in the past.

"Her name?" His question, uttered in a disbelieving tone, was directed at Sean.

"How's that?" Sean responded, leaning in as a crack of thunder shook the room.

"Her name, man," he demanded. "What is the lovely pink ribbon's name?"

"Olivia. Don't have the last name, but it's on file."

"That won't be necessary," he uttered in stunned disbelief. He knew the lovely blonde and intended to find out what the hell she was thinking coming here alone. Tossing back the dregs of his scotch, he slammed the glass down on the top of the bar and stepped away.

He felt the men's eyes on him. "Something wrong?" Jonas asked.

A colossal understatement, to be sure. Most assuredly, something was wrong.

Without answering Jonas, he moved forward through the teeming crowd. He felt like his head was going to explode such was his amazement. For three years, she'd sat outside his office door, quite literally at his beck and call, efficiently following his directives, bending over backward to please him, calling him sir while he nursed a perpetual hard-on. He thought she was efficient and professional, not submissive.

Dammit! Why hadn't he recognized what was beneath his very nose?

Of course, he'd noticed her beauty. Her thick, glossy hair, the full pink lips that she kept slick with gloss, and her stunning figure. With the snug skirts she wore hugging her curves, how could he not notice? Especially when she bent over to get a file or like earlier that afternoon when she retrieved her purse from the bottom drawer and the material had pulled tight across her hips and that full, round, spankable ass.

It suddenly hit him, as sure as his cock lengthened in his trousers. He had noticed all of that, but not consciously. He'd suppressed a lifetime of dominant urges all this time. The question remained, why?

But he could reflect on his cluelessness later. Right now, his mission was to get to her in the throng of bodies because something was definitely wrong here, many things in fact. Foremost, that Olivia had driven two hours in the pouring rain, in her piece-of-shit car, most likely. The one he'd had to jump-start for her twice in the last month. That she'd come alone to an unfamiliar club—a sex club of all places—which he found beyond reckless and in his mind wholly unacceptable, ranked second. A close third, the pink ribbon she wore, which was intriguing but also left him seething with jealousy that someone else had initiated her into the lifestyle.

Last, it infuriated him that while they were obviously in search of the same thing, neither had the guts or the intelligence to open their eyes and see what was right in front of them for years. That was definitely a terrible wrong and one he was determined to put to rights. Pronto. Or as soon as he maneuvered his way to her side through the mass of wall-to-wall people.

AS THE FIRST SET ENDED, Livia sat back, thoroughly enjoying herself and the remains of her giant-size strawberry margarita. With the band on break, the bone-jarring decibel level had decreased to one more conducive to conversation, giving the women at her table an opportunity for introductions.

"Olivia, let me acquaint you with the owners' girls. Megan is with Cap," Mara said, idly waving her hand at the beautiful curvy blonde across from her. "And the extremely pregnant redhead next to her is Regan, her twin."

The petite, small-boned woman, who looked decidedly uncomfortable, shifted in her chair as she rubbed her protruding belly. Livia's eyes shifted back and forth between the two women, deciding they looked nothing alike, until Regan yelped and pressed her hand to her belly as the baby made its presence known. When she looked up, her eyes were the same stunning blue, and she flashed a smile identical to her sister's.

"She's married to Master Rick," Mara went on to explain. "Lexie, the sun-kissed brunette across from you is engaged to Master Jonas, who is a genius with ropes. Wait until you see one of their demonstrations—utter sensual perfection. And, last but not least, the ageless blonde wonder on the end is Joanna, who is married to Master Peter." Each woman smiled warmly and nodded in turn. "Elena," Mara continued, again waving a hand, this time toward the vacated stage, "is our resident rock star and belongs to Dex, the club's master dom."

"First timer?" Megan asked with a smile.

"Yeah, I drove two hours and almost didn't get in. A bunch of girls behind me got turned away."

"How disappointing for them," Regan murmured as she shifted restlessly. "I hope they made it to their cars before the deluge hit."

"The rain had let up when I arrived, but from the wind and the lightning, I think we're in for another round."

"Thank goodness you made it in. Where are you from, Olivia?" Joanna inquired.

"Call me Livia, please. All my friends do. I'm from Austin."

Mara refilled her drink from the pitcher. "Since you're here on an open sub night, bedecked with a ribbon, it's not a stretch to conclude what you're looking for. We have a single dom from Austin."

"Isn't Master J from Austin?" Regan asked, leaning forward this time and grimacing. The poor girl looked and acted miserable.

Megan shook her head. "I don't know. She looks too sweet for Master J."

The name was familiar, the girl out front having the same negative reaction.

"That's the second time I've heard his name mentioned in a not so positive light," Livia blurted out. "Is he a hulking brute or something?"

They all turned to Mara as if she had the answer.

"You're asking me?" she replied with a laugh. "How would I know?"

"You know him better than anyone else," Megan prompted-ed.

"I know him professionally, not as a submissive."

"He's tall, dominant, and yummy, but also rather strait-laced and buttoned up." The other girls laughed, the joke going over Livia's head. "He's quite the enigma. Tell us what you do know," Regan urged.

"The sub grapevine reports that when he plays, he's rather strict and partial to the cane." She paused for a moment, her expression turning pensive while biting her lower lip. "Personally, I found him rather hard to get a handle on. Fortyish, handsome, and extremely tall, taller than Lil T and Tony, even. He's extremely intelligent, full of confidence, but not in an obnoxious sort of way, and has a wonderfully vibrant infectious laugh. That he wraps it all up in a fuddy-duddy tweed suit, wire-framed glasses, and, occasionally, a bow tie throws off my calculations. When Joseph represented me last year, I nicknamed him the swaggering nerd." Her hand flew up to cover her grin. "I probably shouldn't have mentioned that. He's really not a nerd. More like..." She paused a moment before coming up with, "Conservative. Yes. That's a good adjective for him, better yet, old-fashioned."

Livia stiffened, her stomach doing a flip-flop.

No! It couldn't possibly be her Joseph.

"What do you do for a living, Olivia?" Lexie asked. "Maybe you have something in common with Master Joseph. He's an attorney."

"Oh, my god!" Livia bolted out of her chair, knocking it over. "Are you by chance referring to Joseph Hooks?"

Mara stood, too. "That's him. Do you know him?"

"Oh, my god!" she repeated, as her eyes darted frantically around the room.

"I'll take that as a yes," Mara drawled.

"She's gone white as a sheet," Lexie remarked with concern. "Maybe you should sit back down."

Mara ignored Lexie's suggestion and pressed the newcomer for more information, although she wrapped a supportive hand around her arm as she did. "How do you know our Master Joseph?"

"I freaking work for him." Panic had entered her voice, which had risen a full octave. "Merciful heavens! He can't see me here. I've gotta go."

She whirled and started pushing her way through the crowd, her focus on the front doors.

"Olivia, wait," Mara called after her.

She didn't slow or look back, having only one goal in mind, getting out of the club unseen. When she pushed through the heavy double doors and entered the lobby, thunder rumbled long and loud. There was a man at the desk she hadn't noticed on the way in. Dressed in all black, the snug T-shirt he wore had "Rossi Security" written in gold letters across his left pec.

"It's a gully washer out there, miss," he cautioned. "You'll need to wait until it slows."

Disregarding his warning and refusing to be waylaid by the weather, she started for her only means of escape. "I need to go. Now."

When she pulled the heavy doors open, wind and rain assailed her, the force of both ripping the handles from her grasp. Immediately, she moved to close them, struggling against the torrent's sustained force when large male hands appeared next to her smaller ones and easily pushed the doors shut.

"I'm sorry," she gasped, leaning against the doors, already feeling the chill from the drenching as the A/C wafted over her wet skin. "I had no idea it was storming so badly."

Livia turned back to the security guard to further her apology for not listening. Only it wasn't the guard whose hands curled around her upper arms. It wasn't his black T-shirt-clad chest that filled her vision, either. Instead, she stared at a burgundy vest and a gray-check tweed jacket.

Following it upward, she encountered a perfectly knotted gray tie, a clean-shaven, tightly clenched jaw, and full, sensuous lips set in a hard line. She stopped there, knowing who she'd find if she went farther. Closing her eyes tightly, she prayed for the power of teleportation as her face burned.

"Olivia."

His voice, usually a mellow tenor, rang sharp like a hammer forging steel.

"Look at me, little one."

The endearment he'd used with her before but only outside the office in high-stress situations. Like when her mother passed two years back or the time she'd had a debilitating case of the flu and he'd dropped by her apartment to check on her. The pet name, common to the lifestyle, hadn't registered then. Now, using it as a dominant with an errant sub, its meaning rang through loud and clear. He was in charge and she was in big trouble.

She swallowed hard. With the giant doors and severe weather on one side and Joseph on the other, she felt trapped, like a mouse in a maze. Dear heavens!

"I won't ask again."

With his tone deep and uncompromising, she responded as though she had no will.

She looked up into his familiar green eyes. As they gazed intently down at her with more fire than she'd ever seen, she got dizzy. Maybe it was the alcohol or the stress of coming here all alone, or it could be low blood sugar because she'd skipped dinner, much too nervous to eat. No matter the cause, her world turned on end.

Her legs got all wobbly, and she tumbled right into Joseph Hooks' arms, the head honcho at Hooks, Jeffers, and Mahoney, her boss, her dream dom, and the secret love of her life. Then Olivia did something she'd never done in her entire thirty-eight years. She fainted dead away.

Chapter 4

FROM ACROSS THE ROOM, he watched her wake, her eyes blinking open and staring at the unfamiliar ceiling overhead. Suddenly, she winced, her hand coming to her forehead to rub away what had to be a headache, as her delicate brows gathered together. Pink lips, usually soft and curved in a smile, were downturned as she grimaced and sat up in bed.

She looked down at the expansive king-size bed, her hand flaring out and smoothing over what he knew to be soft, sumptuous, mega-thread count sheets. Her head swung up and her eyes swept over the room. When she located him seated casually in a high-backed chair in the corner, her eyes flew wide and her cheeks, usually a lovely peaches and cream, flooded with crimson. She glanced away, looking everywhere except at him.

"Feeling better?" He tried to keep his voice even and not give away the mix of amusement and lust he was feeling, but he wasn't sure he'd succeeded when her face scrunched up a bit.

"Fit as a fiddle, thank you," she lied. Then she pushed aside the covers as she announced, "I should go."

The echo of her words hadn't faded when a loud crack of thunder made her jump. A flash of lightning followed immediately electrifying the air in the room.

"You're not going anywhere tonight." He stood and crossed to the bed. Using his full height to impart his authority, he stood close to the edge, staring down at her, his arms crossed imposingly over his chest. "I asked a question and this time I would like a truthful response."

She glanced up at him briefly, her eyes reaching no farther than his chest then darted away, moving down to her tightly clasped hands in her lap. "I have a bit of a headache is all, sir. Truly, I'm fine."

"How many cocktails did you have this evening?" As he posed his question, he crossed to the bathroom.

"One, but it was very large," was her faint reply as he found aspirin in the medicine cabinet and filled a glass with water from the tap. He strode to her side and held them out for her, palm up.

"Aspirin," he explained succinctly. "Take them without fuss, please."

When she swallowed them down with only a small sip, he ordered further, "Finish it."

Not hesitating in obeying this time, she downed the entire contents. He set her empty glass on the nightstand then sat on the edge of the bed, close alongside her, his thigh pressing fully against hers. Leaning forward, he set his fists on the soft mattress, bracketing her hips, which brought his face very near hers.

With him in her space, she had nowhere to go but flat on her back in the bed. Being vulnerable beneath him clearly not part of her plan, she scooted up toward the headboard and could retreat no farther. Her eyes darted about the room, once again looking for an escape, but his body had cut off all exit routes.

Left without options, she lifted her chin, eyes boldly meeting his.

"It's late, you've been drinking, and there is a flash flood warning out until morning. That's a dangerous combination, which you won't be risking, not on my watch. We'll be spending the night."

She bristled. "Exactly when did it become your watch, sir?"

"The minute you walked into Club Decadence with your hair loose and gleaming like satin, wearing a dress meant to entice, in search of a dom. Tonight, I am that dom, Olivia. No other."

He leaned in and, without making contact, forced her back until she was lying on the pillows. Her hands moved to his chest automatically as he hovered over her, his upper body containing hers. But she didn't resist when his lips lowered to hers, drawn to them as if by an invisible force, with a magnetism he could no longer deny.

She whispered, "Don't I get a say?"

"Certainly, you get to say yes."

He took her mouth, her sweet and savory taste exploding on his tongue as it swept inside. Her lips on his were like feeding on ambrosia, as he'd always guessed they would be.

His hand tangled in her silky hair while the other slid around her back and pulled her body tight against his. He deepened the kiss, plundering her mouth greedily, and continuing in that mode until she whimpered softly in her throat.

Joseph lifted his head a mere fraction so that his lips brushed against hers as he spoke. "That was a sample, little one. Do you want more?"

"Yes, please."

Her husky, breathy, and purely sensual response sent a jolt of need to his already rigid cock. Yet, he wanted to make his offer clear. "Say, 'yes, please, I want more, sir,' and we have a verbal contract for the night."

"If I say no?" she asked, with a hitch in her trembling voice.

"If that is truly what you want, pet, give me your safeword, and this stops right now. But I don't think you drove two hours in a storm to get here tonight only to spend it alone." When she hesitated, he urged, "Be brave and grab hold of what you want, Olivia, with both hands."

Something flashed in the beautiful blue orbs gazing up at him, and there was no hitch or trembling when she replied, "Yes, please. I want much more, sir. Please accept my submission."

Forgetting her momentary uncertainty, his lips curved up in a slow smile. "It will be my absolute pleasure to claim it, and you, pet."

AFTER WONDERING FOR what seemed like forever what his lips would feel like, reality far exceeded her dreams. The heat of Joseph's mouth covering hers was incredible, adding a scorching intensity to the kiss. His tongue swirled and stroked, robbing her of breath. As he trailed his lips down her throat, he tugged down the scooped neckline of her dress and grazed along the upper curves of her breasts. She arched her back, offering him more, wanting with a desperate need his mouth on the hard, aching peaks.

Her fingers, itching to at last learn its texture, sank into the thickness of his hair. He gave her that, but only for a moment before his hands caught her wrists and moved them above her head.

"Can you leave these here for me, pet? Or do I need to help you be good by restraining you?"

She whimpered in her throat, the choice impossible to make. She wanted to touch him, to run her hands not only through his hair but over his skin, to feel the rippling muscles that his dress shirts had hinted at, and the hardness of his thighs and ass that his suit pants couldn't entirely conceal. But she yearned to be bound by him, too. How many times had she imagined being under his command, obeying his dictates, and pleasing him in whatever explicitly naughty way he demanded?

He must have sensed her indecision because he wrapped the conveniently provided cuffs at the center of the headboard around her wrists, choosing for her. Once he had her secure, he dragged his hands down her arms slowly, his touch creating goose bumps as a shiver encompassed her body.

"You're a beautiful woman, Olivia, but like this, bound, submissive, and under my control, you take my breath away," he murmured, before capturing her lips.

"Joseph... sir," she groaned, jerking at her wrists, instinctively testing the limits of the straps connecting her cuffs to the embedded eyebolts in the wood. There was some play in them, but she wasn't going anywhere, not until he decided it would happen.

Groaning, he moved from her mouth, his lips leaving a scorching trail of wetness as they traversed her jaw, down the side of her neck to her chest. The husky, sexy sounds coming from his throat made it clear his need was just as strong as her own.

Then his lips were gone, and he rose above her. With urgent hurried movements, he jerked off his tie and practically tore off his shirt. Standing beside the bed briefly, he stripped the rest of his clothes and Livia's hungry gaze consumed every inch of him he exposed.

The tweed and linen of his wardrobe had done a fine job concealing the whipcord lean muscle making up his long frame. And his easy strength, which he proved by effortlessly flipping her onto her belly, before she got a good look at what she had fantasized about for so long. She felt her zipper give beneath his fingers as he tugged it down. When the material parted, he treated her to a long lick from his searing tongue up her spine.

She expected him to pull the silk from her shoulders and peel it down her hips and legs. Instead, he raised the hem until it rested high on her waist. The next instant, he lowered her panties until they came to rest at the top of her thighs. Pulling her up on her knees, he palmed her full cheeks and squeezed.

"Exquisite," he murmured, the single word a rush of hot breath over the dampness of her intimate flesh. It was nothing compared to the sear of his tongue when his thumbs spread her open and he licked the length of her pussy.

He didn't lift his mouth and vibrations rippled through her when he hummed, "Mmm, as fucking sweet as I knew you would be."

Olivia's cries rent the air, growing louder when his tongue focused on her clit, circling and flicking and sucking. He stayed there for several minutes, sending her to the brink of orgasm, but just as she was about to soar over the edge, he moved higher and plunged into her drenched channel.

Her fingers curled around the restraining straps that prevented her from touching him. If she were free, she would have pulled his face closer, with his mouth centered on her clit, and held it there until delivered on the climax his lips and talented tongue had promised. But she could only hang on, moaning in frustration as he moved farther away, continuing inexorably upward, to her small rear opening, and gave it a wet glide with his tongue.

She groaned because that felt as wonderful as it did naughty.

The bed shifted as Joseph sat back, and he resumed the slow, deep massage of her bottom.

"You have an ass made for spanking, with your satiny-smooth skin and creamy complexion. I can imagine how lovely it would look with a blush of pink. The same as the ribbon you wear. You have some experience as a submissive. Can I presume you have been spanked before?"

"Yes, sir," she answered between panting breaths.

"With more than a hand?" he asked as he kneaded her flesh slowly.

She moaned, her head bobbing up and down in answer.

"Perhaps with a paddle, a flogger, and a cane?"

"Yes, to all except the last, sir."

"Hmm," he hummed, diving back in for another long lick from clit to ass, the vibrations which she now suspected he did on purpose, making her back arch as she canted her hips and parted her thighs seeking more. "The cane is an underutilized and unappreciated implement, to be sure. I'd like to see this ass colored with a few stripes."

The thought of the long, narrow bamboo or rattan rod snapping sharply against her bottom, leaving marks placed there by Joseph's will and design, a tangible sign of his possession sent a rush of liquid heat to her pussy. Near mad with desire, she rocked back against his wickedly arousing mouth.

He chuckled softly; the sensation sending a shiver up her spine.

"Please, sir," she gasped.

"That is my aim."

His words coincided with the swat of his hand against the swell of her right cheek. It had been an eternity since her last spanking. For it to be happening again, at last, by Joseph's firm hand, was a fantasy come true. The muscles low in her belly tightened and her clit pulsed with need. A few more and she'd lose control.

When another smack fell, this time on her left cheek, Livia tossed her head back, flipping her hair out of her face, gasping for air as she tried not to come.

Three more, slightly harder, struck in quick succession on one side, followed by a trio of identical swats on the other.

"Joseph, sir, I can't wait."

"You're ready to come already, pet?"

Two upward strokes landed full on the lowermost curve of her cheek, the heel of his hand falling dangerously near her pussy lips. The rippling energy shot straight through to her clit.

"Yes, I can't"—she gasped and swallowed as another upward stroke fell—"hold it back."

A duo of identical upstrokes fell on the other side as he urged, "Don't. I want to see you come apart as I spank your exquisite ass."

He laid into her, then, not overly hard but fast and low enough to catch her sit spots and upper thighs. The repeated blows reverberated through her pussy and the inflamed, hair-trigger nerves inside. He followed that with one smack dead center on her wet lips.

She shuddered violently as her orgasm ripped through her. It went on and on as waves of bliss radiated outward, coursing up her belly to her painfully taut nipples and down her thighs to her toes. All of it emanated from the hand now, focusing directly over her clit as he repeatedly swatted her wet, swollen, and highly sensitized skin.

As her climax receded, the sensation was too much, and she twisted, trying to get away. But he was the dominant and in control of her and her pleasure. His arm snaked around her waist, holding her still. The relentless hand stopped though, replaced by gentle fingers gliding through and into her wetness.

It wasn't long until the need built again.

"Perfect," he murmured as he moved into place behind her. She heard a wrapper crinkle an instant before the smooth head of his cock moved over her sensitive skin. The next instant, he sank into her.

Joseph's cock was commensurate to the rest of him—freaking immense—and stretched her to her limits. He'd prepared her well, though, and despite his above average proportions and how long it had been since she'd been with a man, he sank deep until he filled her completely. The sensations of his body pressed against her tingling, freshly spanked cheeks, being possessed more fully than ever before, and by Joseph, who she'd longed to take her like this for oh-so long, reignited her passion to a fever pitch.

His fingers curved around her hips, holding her still for his possession as he moved inside her. He started out slow and easy, but soon his harsh breathing mingled with her soft moans. Pulling her back to meet each forward thrust, soon, he was pumping furiously. The sound of their skin smacking together echoed loudly throughout the bedroom.

It was glorious, and she couldn't hold off any longer.

When her second climax claimed her, the harsh cries of his first soon followed. The masculine sound of satisfaction washed over her and filled her with warmth. That she could bring him such pleasure pleased her as a woman, but even more so as a submissive.

He stilled, his cock planted deep inside for several bliss-filled seconds, before sliding out a fraction only to return, sheathing and filling her once more. Damp with sweat, her hair clinging to her face, she listened to his rapid breathing behind her.

Smiling in contentment, she reveled in the feel of him, still rigid inside her. Never had she come so hard or felt so utterly dominated before. At that moment, her infatuation and unrequited longing morphed into love. Heck, who was she kidding? It had been love for a very long time.

A nagging thought crept into her consciousness. What if he didn't feel the same?

Joseph pulled out and left the bed, disappearing into the bathroom briefly. When he returned, he rolled her limp form onto her side and spooned against her back. The restraints strained her arms in this position. As his hand rose and checked them, her head tilted to watch.

"Too tight?" he asked.

"No, sir, but the slack is gone. We must have slid down."

Easily, with one arm, he scooted her toward the headboard until her elbows bent and her arms rested comfortably on the pillow in front of her.

"Better?"

"Much. Thank you, sir."

"Good, because the night is young and I'm not nearly done with you yet." To prove his point, he lifted her top leg, bending her knee to her chest. This opened her pussy, and he didn't hesitate to claim it again, entering her in one powerful thrust from behind.

A CAR ENGINE REVVING outside her window awoke her.

When she opened her eyes, Olivia frowned at the gray light coming through the unfamiliar curtains. Either the sun hadn't risen yet, or the storm hadn't abated. When the man at her back stirred, memories of the evening before and the passion-filled night that followed came to her in a rush.

She was pleased to have proven her hypothesis right that behind his staid all-business persona was a voracious, passionate lover. That he also had boundless stamina was an unexpected and very pleasant bonus.

Shifting slightly beneath the covers, Olivia became reacquainted with muscles she hadn't used in sometime. There was a pleasant tenderness between her thighs, a lingering sign of a dominant's possession that hadn't been there in too long a time. Her bottom, currently nestled in the curve of his body, bore none of the sting or heat from his broad hand had created, which she found disappointing. But his arm tightened reflexively around her as the warm hand holding her bare breast did the same, and she smiled. Wasn't this an awesome way to start the day?

Joseph was a cuddler, something she never would have guessed

She wanted to see what he looked like asleep and turned carefully. Without his glasses and with his dark hair that was longish on top and tousled from sleep, he looked years younger, late thirties at most. During the last time he'd taken her, Joseph had removed the cuffs. He also rolled her to her back and with their limbs entwined had taken her in a very vanilla fashion—missionary; a time-honored and always appreciated position—with long, measured strokes while he licked, kissed, and nibbled on her neck and the hard peaks of her breasts.

Free to touch him everywhere, when he'd brought her to climax yet again, she had wrapped her arms around his broad shoulders, the fingers of one hand entwined in the hair at his nape, reveling in its thick silky texture.

Now, as she watched his handsome face, relaxed in sleep, a thick swath of those silken strands fell across his forehead. She was tempted to brush it back but refrained, not ready to face him yet.

Morning-after doubts crept in like the approaching dawn. What happened now? He had mentioned nothing beyond last night. In fact, his statements seemed time limited.

Tonight, I am that dom, and *say yes...and we have a verbal contract for the night.*

What if one night was all he ever intended?

She had invaded his territory after all, arriving unexpectedly and shocking him down to his structured and very organized toes. In the entire time she'd worked for him, she'd never seen him with the same woman twice. Maybe taking a different sub every night was his style here at Club Decadence as well. He was there on open sub night. Perhaps he liked new conquests.

The notion that he would suddenly want her as she wanted him—a committed relationship, marriage, babies, the whole nine yards—after all this time, was as fleeting as a dream.

As she lay there, feeling the weight of what they had done, the impact on her future, her career, her livelihood, pressed heavy like an anvil on her chest. The urge to escape became overwhelming. She eased away, inching her legs toward the side of the bed as she slowly slid out from under his arm.

When he stirred, Livia held her breath as she watched anxiously, waiting for those long lashes to part and surprise her with the ever-changing color behind them, but he rolled onto his side, his back to her.

A mixture of disappointment and relief rushed through her. She hesitated only a moment before going into action, easing off the bed and, in a blink, gathering her clothes. With shoes in hand and still awkwardly zipping her dress up the back, she was out the door, closing it quietly behind her.

Finding herself in a long, thankfully empty, corridor, she looked frantically around, trying to get her bearings. Since Joseph had carried her there unconscious, she hadn't a clue which way to go. With a fifty-fifty shot, she turned left, praying she wouldn't run into anyone. But at the same time, she longed for Joseph to appear at her side, uttering words of love and commitment as he scooped her up in his arms and carried her back to their bed.

Neither happened, and she made it to the stairwell at the end of the hall and quickly descended on soundless bare feet. Two flights down, she pushed open a metal door and stepped out into the nearly abandoned parking lot. When she did, a lone ray of sunlight broke through the clouds, falling upon her like an accusing finger. Two steps into her walk of shame—something she hadn't done since her reckless early twenties—the door clanged shut behind her with ominous finality.

Chapter 5

HER HANDS TREMBLED as she lifted her mug to her lips and sipped her coffee. Although two was usually her limit, it was her fourth of the morning. But after her trip home at daybreak, driving through more severe weather, she was a wreck, and it was too early for shots of bourbon.

The two-hour trip had taken three. With torrential rains and high winds sweeping across the highway, visibility had reduced to about ten feet. She could barely make out the brake lights of the car in front of her. Not helping matters, the tears that just wouldn't stop.

Setting her mug aside, she stared at her laptop, the glaring whiteness of the blank document unchanged since she pulled it up two hours ago. She glanced at the small clock in the corner of the screen. Had he made it into work?

It was approaching 8:30 when she called the office, leaving Joseph a voice mail—her second cowardly act of the day—that she wasn't feeling well and wouldn't be in, taking a personal day. Her only task she faced today, other than coming to grips with the colossal stupidity of having sex with her boss, updating her resume.

She couldn't concentrate, however, imagining his reaction when she woke and found her gone. Maybe he'd been relieved that the stilted morning-after dialogue wouldn't be necessary, or concerned that she'd simply disappeared—they weren't strangers after all—or possibly angry that she'd robbed him of the opportunity for a morning quickie before giving her the old heave ho?

With a long, drawn-out sigh, she laid her head on the table. How had she messed up her life so badly in a single night?

A loud knock—actually, it was several in quick succession—sounded at the door.

She jolted upward, her eyes burning into the wood as if she could see who was on the other side if she tried hard enough. Even if it were possible, x-ray vision was unnecessary when she knew without a doubt who it was. The raps repeated, louder.

"Olivia," Joseph's stern tone cut through the solid wood door. "Open up."

She didn't dare move or breathe.

"I know you're home. Your car is in its space."

On shaky legs, she stood, compelled to do as both her ex-dom and soon to be ex-boss said.

"Now, Olivia."

Her stocking feet padded quietly to the door. As she reached for the dead bolt, her hand trembled. She fisted it to quell its shaking. Staring at the brass lock, she continued to hesitate.

"Joseph—" she began softly, but his unyielding command interrupted.

"I won't have a discussion through a door. I also won't tell you again. Open up right now."

With trembling fingers, she turned the dead bolt, released the chain, and twisted the lock on the end of the doorknob in sequence. When she pulled the door open and looked up at him, her jaw dropped. His hair stood up in a riot of angles, as if he'd run his fingers through it. A day's growth of beard shadowed his chin. In shirtsleeves and no tie, wearing the same clothes he'd worn the day before, he was a mussed, wrinkled mess. Never had she seen him in this condition.

It occurred to her, suddenly, that he must have come directly to her from San Antonio.

"Move aside and let me in," he said in a low growl. "Unless you want your neighbors to hear me chewing you a new one."

She blinked in stunned surprise then backed up a step as Joseph prowled forward. Once he cleared it, he slammed it shut with a thud. Then, like an enraged tiger and she his prey, he stalked her. She kept pace, matching him step-by-step in retreat. His eyes, an angry forest green, blazed down at her, unwavering, even when he shut the door behind him with a decisive slam.

"In all my years as a dominant, no submissive has ever ditched me in the middle of the night. Not only does it wound my pride, Olivia, but coming from you, it stings. What did you think that was, a one-night stand?"

She had the good grace to flush, heat suffusing her face clear to her ears.

"You did," he accused, his jaw clenched in outrage. "What's going on in that head of yours? You know me. Do you really believe I'd treat you in such a manner?"

Still backing up, she came to a sudden halt, unable to go farther when the back of her legs bumped up against the arm of her couch.

"Joseph, I—"

"No," he bit out. "I don't want to hear your excuses. I'm here to finish what we started last night. Do you know why?"

She shook her head, afraid to say a word.

"Because a session with me does not end until I say it does." He pulled her up by the arms, his long fingers firm but not hurtful. "Perhaps I missed it. Did you say red, by chance?"

"No, sir," she breathed out, barely above a whisper.

His hands went to the belt in her jeans, unbuckled it, and in one long pull, zipped it from the loops.

"Do you have a different safeword you failed to disclose?"

As he spoke, he spun her to face the couch. Gathering her wrists in one hand, he bound them behind her back, using her own belt as a restraint.

"Orchid, sir."

"Your favorite flower," he murmured as his long body leaned into hers, his thighs pressing against the back of her own. His hips pinned her in place, holding her still, while the hard length of him pressed against her bound hands.

"It is," she gasped, "but—"

"I would have remembered had you said it. But you didn't, did you?"

He pulled up her T-shirt, his hands cupping her breasts from behind, lifting and massaging them.

"No, sir. I'm—"

"Silence."

The single word, said in an even but steely tone, sent a sharp jolt of fire, like a streak of lightning straight through to her clit. When his fingers curled into the cups of her bra and pulled them down, she could barely think. And, when his thumbs and index fingers found the taut peaks and rolled them, pinching them deliciously, she could barely breathe.

"You do not have permission to speak, except to say your safeword. Red or orchid—whichever you choose. I will honor both."

He paused, clearly giving her time to say one of them now. Left breathless by his forcefulness, her body too aroused by his dominance, Livia let the seconds tick by without a response. She knew her time was over when his fingers found the button on her jeans. With the zipper undone, he yanked down her pants, panties and all, then he bent her over the high, over-stuffed arm of her couch.

Two fingers dipped into her wetness, easily located her center, and plunged inside. The only acknowledgment he gave her blatant arousal was a grunt before his other hand came down hard on her ass. This wasn't the sensual spanking of hours before when he was pleased with her. No, this was without a doubt punishment.

Her head reared back, and she sucked in a gulp of air as another blast of fire rained down on her ass. That's when she saw herself—hair wild about her head, lips parted as she panted fast, shirt shoved up to her shoulders, breasts bare and pushed up wantonly by her lowered bra. The image reflected in the sliding glass door was the embodiment of a conquered and dominated woman. And it didn't include what she couldn't see; her jeans and panties in a twist around her knees.

Mesmerized, she watched as his hand rose and fell repeatedly, keeping up a steady pace, building an intense burn with each stroke of his broad palm, not only on her skin but low in her belly and within the achy place between her thighs.

"After years working alongside one another, forty-plus hours per week, attending countless business and social functions together, I thought we had deeper feelings—respect, trust, esteem—at the very least." He didn't allow her time to answer, moving to the tops of her thighs to apply swat after scorching swat. "Since you obviously missed it, let me make it clear. Last night was beyond boss and employee, much more than friends, and a damn sight more than a casual fling. Last night took us to an entirely different level. I claimed you, Olivia. Therefore, your response this morning, running from me, was altogether objectionable."

He grunted again, still whaling away, peppering her ass and thighs with fiery heat.

"For leaving without a word, sneaking off like a college co-ed after a drunken mistake, for that bit of rudeness alone, you deserve more than my hand." He stopped, leaned over her back, and pressed his lips to her ear. "Don't you dare move."

He followed it up with a lick along the delicately curved shell and a quick nip on the lobe. Then he strode away.

She heard him rummaging around in the kitchen. Her mind did a hasty inventory of what he might find as a punishment tool—wooden spoons, spatulas in all sizes, a plastic cutting board with a handle—any of them would drive his point home.

She shouldn't have left without speaking to him. A shiver coursed through her body as she remembered his words. *I claimed you*.

How was she supposed to know that? He hadn't said a word, had he? She was replaying every moment in her brain when the creak of the floorboards announced his return.

At that moment, it clicked. *I am that dom, Olivia. No other.*
She winced, calling herself an oblivious fool and worse.

"Joseph, please, may I speak?"

"No," he barked.

She bit her lip. He had never been this stern or angry with her—ever. Of course, she'd never left him naked in bed after a night of unbelievable sex, either.

"Obviously, we have particulars to work out, so I'll ask to be clear. Do you accept my authority to punish you, pet?"

"You're angry, Joseph. Maybe this isn't the best time."

"I'm not angry. I'm pissed the hell off, but I'm in control or I wouldn't be here. Now, give me your answer. Do you accept my right to punish you for your abysmal behavior?"

"I—"

"A simple yes or no, sir, is all that is required."

"Yes, sir."

"Excellent. No need to count."

A *swish* sounded and a line of scorching heat blazed a trail across her ass from cheek to cheek. She cried out, teetering forward on her precarious perch as much from surprise as from the blistering switch, cane, or whatever the heck it was he'd found in her kitchen.

His hand on her lower back steadied her. "You will receive five more strokes. At that point, if your striped ass has appeased me enough to discuss this, we will. If not, you'll get a half dozen more."

Another *swish* preceded more fire. "Ow, ow, ow!"

"Four more."

A hiss followed the next stroke as she sucked in air between her teeth at the searing sting it ignited. Spaced evenly apart, he allowed each blow to flare to a fiery burn. Somehow, he knew when the sting eased a bit, only then did the next one land.

As he did with every task, he worked with precision, moving from the top down, covering her entire ass, careful that no strokes forged the same path. When the count was at two, her moan changed to a low keening as the stick—or cane, or whatever the fuck—fell across the crease between her cheek and thigh.

The sixth and final stroke followed shortly, applied an inch below the last, landing on the fleshy part of her thighs. Those last two hurt worst of all.

"Please, Joseph," she cried out, tears flowing. They were more from shame, however, although the burn gracing her ass and thighs deserved honorable mention at least. "Forgive me. I acted rashly, inexcusably, and you're right. Out of esteem and respect for you, I owed you so much more."

The implement fell on the cushion in front of her. She recognized it as the plastic wand from her mini-blinds in the kitchen. As she pictured her bottom marked with his stripes, a fire rivaling the one on her ass stirred to life in her pussy.

He moved behind her, no longer towering over her prostrate form but crouching, his face level with her well-chastised bottom. Joseph's hands brushed softly over her inflamed cheeks, his mouth spreading gentle kisses in their wake. When his fingers found her drenched with arousal, his lips grazed her heated skin.

"You're soaking wet," he groaned against her hot skin. "I must have you again."

"Take me, master, please." Belatedly, she realized her error. He hadn't approved for her to call him that yet. With a name tacked on out in the club, it was expected, but privately, it was special, usually reserved for a committed couple. But in this instance, it seemed right and had come freely from her lips.

Thankfully, he didn't correct her. Instead, he tilted her backward until her feet touched the floor. Hurriedly, he stripped her jeans and panties down and off. Pushing to his feet, he curled his hand under her knee and cocked it until it rested high along the back of the couch, spreading her unbelievably wide.

A second passed, enough for the crinkle of foil as he gloved up, then his cock thrust into her, bottoming out with the first penetration. With an arm around her waist, the other slid around her chest, grasping the opposite shoulder. He raised her upper body, not upright but at the perfect angle to pump inside her—long, hard, deep—his hips and thighs slapping against her tenderized and punished skin with each thrust.

It was possession, pure and simple. Bound, helpless, spread open for the taking, she had no control and didn't want any. She wanted Joseph to have total control. Never had she experienced the overwhelming need to submit. Not in years with Vaughn, or with the two doms she'd been with before him. Only in her fantasies had she a dom mastered her so completely—those dreams starring one man.

His hands swept over her belly and breasts. One lingered to roll and tug on a nipple, while the other slid up her chest to her throat. When his hand cupped her jaw, angling her face up and back, he demanded more. "Give me your mouth, pet."

With his tongue possessing above and his cock firmly embedded below, he pumped into her relentlessly, pushing her toward a looming peak. She was about to soar over the summit when he withdrew. Her orgasm seemingly so close became like an elusive mirage just out of reach. Her cries of frustration filled the room.

His next order sounded in a gruff but determined voice. "Kneel."

He had to help her up from her awkward position then, on rubbery legs, and with less than her usual grace, she knelt before him. Joseph's hand fisted in her hair and guided her head back as he brought his cock to her lips. Without being told to, she opened, greedily accepting him as he slid along her tongue.

"Suck," he demanded.

Her lips immediately closed around him. He glided into her once, twice, and a final time, which is when, with a ferocious growl, he came on her tongue and down her throat. Both hands were in her hair, cradling her head, while Livia lapped and licked him, his body trembling as he came down from his climax. After several long, intimate moments, he withdrew.

"I'm due in Ft. Worth this afternoon, as you know. I'll be back on Saturday at eleven o'clock. That leaves you approximately forty-eight hours to think about what you want and make a decision."

Behind her, she heard the rustle of denim, a distinctive zipping, and the clink of his belt buckle. With her body still humming with arousal and yearning for him, she closed her eyes and suppressed a groan. He was demonstrating his control of her and her pleasure by denying both.

Joseph squatted in front of her, his large hands sliding up to her cheeks, lifting her face so close to his she could feel his breath. Wanting him so badly her teeth ached, she leaned into his touch.

"You have two choices. Forget about last night and go back to the way we were. Working together on friendly terms but tamping down your desires and living in self-denial because you're afraid to go for what you want." Gently stroking a finger down her cheek, he met her shimmering blue eyes. "Or, you can come to me at three o'clock and surrender, to both the pleasure of last night and, when needed, the discipline of this morning, fulfilling your long-suppressed desires and living your life as you're meant to. Not merely going through the motions, but experiencing it at its fullest, with me."

He moved closer, his lips brushing hers as he spoke.

"But I warn you, pet. I'll accept no half measures. If you choose surrender, you will do so on your knees."

His lips and the sweep of his tongue as he claimed her mouth in full measure, proving in no uncertain terms what he meant smothered her gasp of both excitement and alarm.

After several heated, hungry moments of a kiss that embodied possession, he stood. His hand under her jaw tilted her face up to his.

"Now, little one, on my terms, this session is at an end."

He moved toward the door, his footsteps nearly drowned out by the pounding of her pulse in her ears.

"One more thing, pet," he said softly from across the room. "No touching. When you come to me, I want you as you are now: cunt bare, gloriously wet, and hungry for me."

With his decree given, he left her. It wasn't until the door thumped shut in his wake that she realized he had released her bound wrists. That's when she wilted, sagging limply against the side of the couch. Her body still humming from his touch and aching with need. Livia wished for the power to call him back and tell him she didn't need more time to think and decide. She already knew what she would be doing at three o'clock two days from now.

Chapter 6

"TELL ME EVERYTHING, and don't you dare leave out a single detail."

Olivia regarded her friend from the doorstep for a moment before greeting her politely. "Yes, I'm fine, Emma. Thank you for asking. I appreciate your concern. Would I like to come in and take off my jacket before I spill my guts? Don't mind if I do. And a glass of wine would be wonderful, too."

Color flooded Emma's cheeks as she glanced at David, who simply grinned while shaking his head. "Sorry," she uttered softly.

"C'mon in, sugar," David offered where his overeager wife had not. Moving forward, he kissed her cheek and then helped her out of her lightweight jacket.

"It's wet," she warned. The rain had continued all day, perpetuating her gloomy mood.

"How about that glass of wine you mentioned? You might need it, since Em's intent on raking you over the coals."

With a tilt of her head, Livia eyed her friend who appeared ready to burst at the seams with curiosity. She couldn't resist teasing. "If I knew I was coming to an interrogation, I'd have brought a rubber hose."

"All right, you two, I apologized. I can't help that I've been dying to hear about Club Decadence from someone who has actually been." Emma grabbed her hand and dragged her over to the couch. "Do they really have gold-plated fixtures and marble floors? Were the Decadence masters as smoking hot as everyone claims? And the giant playroom, tell me about that. Did they fuck openly in a free-for-all BDSM-style orgy?"

"Emma!" her husband chastised sharply with a grimace. A dom himself, he didn't tolerate crude language from his submissive wife, unless they were playing, when, according to Emma, both of them could get pretty salty.

"Sorry, babe." She flashed him her dimples, which earned her a warning look.

"Can you behave while I get Livia a glass of wine?" he asked.

"I'll try really hard, sir."

He grunted. "It will take a miracle, I'm afraid."

To ease the sting of his words, he kissed the top of her head before disappearing into the kitchen.

"Okay," she immediately whispered. "Now that the big bad dom is gone, give me the dirt."

Livia tried to answer her questions in order. "Let's see. First, I honestly didn't notice the fixtures or the floors. Second, yes, I didn't see them all, but the ones I did were to-die-for hot. And third, again, I don't know because I never made it past the bar to the dungeon. But the third-floor apartments are very nice."

Emma's smile faded, and she blinked. "Wait! Apartments? No one said anything about apartments." She paused a moment, her brain clearly struggling to process the information as she added, "And back up a minute. How could you go and not see the dungeon? Did you chicken out?"

"No. I met someone."

Emma's shock and bewilderment were instantly swept aside and replaced with a wide grin. "Awesome! Did you finally get laid?"

"Emma Jean, that is enough!" David barked on his way back in with three glasses of wine held easily in one hand.

After murmuring another apology for being crude, she turned wide eyes on Livia. "Let me rephrase. Did you sleep with him?"

Her face was already hot, but it went up in flames, which was answer enough.

"Hot damn, you did!" Emma looked at David with wide eyes, ignoring his heavy sigh as she repeated, "She met someone." Turning back to Livia, she demanded, "Tell me all about him. Is he a hunky Green Beret, too?"

"Not quite. I think he's hunky, but not in a mountainous, rugged Green Beret kind of way. He's tall and lean, built more like a swimmer than John Rambo, and very smart, and—"

"Good in bed? Did the room even have a bed? Or did you do it on some fancy piece of bondage equipment?"

Livia opened her mouth to reply, but her eyes shifted to David and she stopped.

"Don't mind me," he said, unfazed. "People tell me about their sex lives all the time during therapy."

As a clinical psychologist, he must have heard all manner of outrageous things, sex included. Besides, he was a dom himself and she'd known him forever. Shrugging off her concerns for what was proper, she admitted, "Yes, there was a very nice comfortable bed and *good* doesn't do the sex justice."

Her friend practically vibrated with excitement. "What does it justice? Great?" Emma held her hands up about eight inches apart. "Fantastic? Magnificent? Humongous?" With each word, she moved them farther apart until she had her hands at a ridiculous—and humanly impossible—distance from each other.

Both Emma and Livia burst into laughter as David, playing the put-upon husband, grabbed his wife's hands and pulled them down. "You are both incorrigible."

"Seriously, give me the deets," her friend pleaded.

"I won't go into size specifications—"

"Bless you," David interjected.

"But," Livia went on as though he hadn't interrupted, "the experience was great, magnificent, and fantastic, all of that and more. It was also potentially life-altering because there's a problem. I've known him for years."

Emma gasped. "You're kidding. Who is it?"

"Joseph Hooks."

This time Emma's jaw practically dropped to the floor, and her eyes got as big as moons. For once, she was speechless.

David, who had taken a seat beside her, reached over and with a finger beneath her chin, closed her mouth for her. That seemed to snap her out of it.

"Joseph is a dom?"

"Very much so," Livia replied. "Who knew?"

Emma shook her head in denial, but David promptly raised his hand. She turned to her husband. "How would you know? You've never met him."

"Darlin', I've listened to Livia go on about the man for three years. He's intelligent, self-disciplined, a natural leader, emerging at the top of his field in short order. Where so many attorneys turn smug and egocentric, he has clearly risen above that and maintained his self-respect and his regard for others."

"You got all that from what I've said?" Livia asked in amazement. "Are you a psychologist or an FBI profiler?"

He chuckled. "Often that's one and the same. Although, it doesn't take a PhD to know he's a dominant when I know you are submissive. You wouldn't be attracted to him otherwise."

"Why didn't you say something?" Emma demanded. "If she knew her boss was a dom, it would have saved her a lot of lost time and frustration."

"I believe love must find its own way, as you know."

Her friend's eyes rolled toward the ceiling, and she sighed. "In David-speak, that means he's anti-matchmaking. So even if he'd told me his impression about Joseph, he would have forbidden me to say a word."

David smiled at his wife's astute summation then turned quizzical eyes on Livia. "What is the problem you mentioned?"

"Other than going to a BDSM club, outing myself to my boss, and then having sex with him?" she asked, as if his IQ had dropped forty points, although in David's case that would have left it still well above normal.

"Yeah, honey," he answered, "other than you went to a fetish club specifically to meet someone and when you did, that someone was the man you've been mooning over for years. On the surface, it sounds like a win-win. So aside from all that, what seems to be the problem?"

Livia recognized the all-too familiar glint in his eye. It usually preceded the offering of a few pearls of wisdom from his unique insight into the human mind.

"This morning," she began, with little arm twisting, knowing that one or the other of them would wheedle it out of her anyway. "When the heat of the moment had passed, I panicked."

"And you ran," David surmised.

She nodded.

"But why?" Emma asked.

"Morning-after doubts overwhelmed me, that and the fact that in all the time I've worked for him, he never made a move. He could have any woman he wants with his wealth, power, and good looks. I convinced myself I was nothing but a piece of ass, an insignificant legal secretary, and that he was only interested in one night."

"Oh, Liv," Em's cry was heartfelt as she reached over and gripped her hand.

"I know; it was stupid. Believe me, he wasn't happy when he arrived at my door this morning."

"I imagine not," David said with a frown. "Did he spank your ass? I would have."

Livia shifted in her seat. Once again, inadvertently through deeds rather than words, giving herself away.

David chuckled. "Sounds like me and Joseph would get along well."

"Why do I do this to myself?" she asked under her breath as she tossed back the rest of her wine.

"Allow me to take a crack at that."

"I can't wait to hear this," Emma whispered, which earned her another warning glare from her husband.

"I'm keeping a mental count, Emma Jean."

She promptly wrinkled her nose but said nothing more. Livia, despite the murkiness of her situation, had to work hard to suppress a giggle.

"In love and romance, Livia dear, as the saying goes, 'sometimes you can't see the forest for the trees.' I'd hazard a guess that Joseph returns your feelings, but his reluctance to express them might have something to do with a little thing called sexual harassment. Power exchange in the lifestyle is consensual, but in the workplace between a boss and his subordinate, it is inherently dangerous. As far as not having made a move, if you think back on your relationship with the perspective you have now, I'm certain you'll find signs you've overlooked."

"He's right, Liv." Emma nodded encouragingly. "He often took you to family and office functions rather than a date, never forgot your birthday, and sent you flowers more times than I can count just to say thank you."

"I thought he was being nice."

"Honey," Emma said with a small laugh. "My boss has never sent me flowers."

"And he better not," David growled. She stroked his forearm as though gentling him, which Livia thought was sweet.

"How did you leave it with him?" she asked. "You being here can't be a good sign."

"He had to go out of town for work, but before he left, he gave me a choice. Rewind and go back to yesterday—status quo—or submit to him when he gets back."

"You're not seriously considering saying no!" Emma cried in outrage. "Olivia Suzanne Wright, don't you dare! You've been gaga over that man since the first day you met him."

"That isn't true. Vaughn had just dumped me. When I met Joseph, I had sworn off men, if you recall."

"Is that what's making you hesitant?" David asked, clearly wearing his PhD hat.

They had been there for her after the breakup and knew all the gory details. She'd been a mess for a while afterward, and David had helped her get back on track, or so she thought, until her insecurities reemerged yesterday morning.

"I thought Vaughn was the one. What if I'm wrong again? I have more to lose now than the last time." Her eyes got misty as she thought of losing both her job and Joseph. "I don't know why I even bother looking for love. I always screw it up. A cat is looking better by the minute."

"That's a rather defeatist attitude, honey," Emma observed gently.

"I don't mean to sound flippant, or rude, but that's easily said when you're sitting with your husband's arm around you."

"Consider this," David offered. "You talk about wanting to find someone, to settle down and start a family, but down deep, because of that bastard Steros, you are afraid of loving and losing again. Therefore, you've turned down good men for dates, found minute flaws, and rejected the ones that you deigned to go out with, and instead, clung to the one consistent relationship you had with a man that was safe—me."

When she and Emma shared a look, her friend nodded. Wow, how pathetic did that make her sound?

"Yet, your need to submit is so great, because that is who you are, you went to a club hoping to find a safe dom to fill the emptiness. Instead, you found Joseph, the man you want the most. Bonus, he's a dom. But he threatened your safe place, and you ran, preferring not to take the risk at all rather than trying and failing at love again."

Astonished by his laser accuracy, she stared at him in awe then gaped at Emma with wide eyes.

"Imagine living with him," she drawled. "He's a dom and an expert in human behavior. I don't stand a chance of putting anything over on him."

David's arm tightened as he pulled her in close. "I don't recommend that you try, baby." From Emma's high-pitched yelp, Livia guessed he'd given her a precautionary pinch.

"So, doc, what is your recommendation?"

"What do you want, Olivia?"

"I want Joseph."

"Then you don't need me to tell you the answer. Do you, honey?"

Chapter 7

SHE QUESTIONED THE wisdom of her pencil skirt for the tenth time in as many minutes as she knelt on the thick rug in the center of his office. The flowing A-line dress with the cutaway jacket she'd tried on first would have made much more sense. But Joseph mentioned liking her snug skirts, and with pleasing him in mind, she'd gone with the impractical.

So here she was with her head bowed, hands behind her back, on her knees with her too-tight skirt bunched up at her hips in order to spread her thighs wide in her submissive pose. Hopefully, the effort would earn her forgiveness points.

She waited. A clock in his office loudly ticked off each passing second. She'd been ten minutes early, but she didn't dare check the time now. As soon as she did, he'd come through the door.

Keys jangling outside the door announced his arrival and instantly kicked her heart into high gear. Without looking up, her eyes cast downward and her body humming with anticipation, she focused on his movements. Hearing the snick of the lock and the soft thud of his shoes on the carpet was enough to pinpoint his location as he crossed to his desk and with a clink, set his keys and probably his phone on the desk. More soft footfalls and his brown Ferragamo loafers came into view, stopping about a foot in front of her. She recognized them instantly, having picked them up with two of his suits from Nordstrom's.

"Your decision pleases me greatly."

"I want to be yours, sir."

"Look at me. I prefer to see those beautiful blue eyes."

Her lashes lifted and her head tilted back until she gazed up at his handsome face. Unlike the stern visage from their last meeting, he looked relaxed, his jaw no longer tightly clenched. Though they burned with intensity, it wasn't anger she saw glittering in the green eyes behind his glasses, and his lips had curved into a gentle smile instead of a scowl.

"Are you ready to surrender?"

"Yes, sir. I've wanted this, and you, since the day we met, but was afraid to admit it until now."

"Brave, pet." His touch was gentle as he ran his hand over her hair, tucking a few stray tendrils behind her ear before his fingers slowly traced along her jaw. "I prefer master when we're in session."

"Yes, master." She smiled. The significance behind the title giving her a warm feeling inside.

"Good girl." His hand fell away and he took a step back. Still close, but no longer touching. "Now, prove you want to be mine. Open your blouse."

His order sent waves of electric pleasure coursing through her body. She would have expected it from the fiery dom of two mornings ago or the naked, passionate dominant of the preceding evening, but this man looked and sounded like the Joseph of old. Respected attorney, upstanding citizen of Austin, who volunteered his time assisting indigent clients a few days each month and regularly gave his free time to help at the local Salvation Army. Each month, she shopped and wrapped gifts for kids living at the shelter who were celebrating a birthday and, if not for Joseph, their special day might pass with nothing at all.

His acts of kindness, though small, were beautiful. He also helped at the annual "Doing the Most Good" fundraiser. She knew this because he had enlisted her help these past few years. That this generous man was the same one who just now asked her to open her blouse in his conservative and very orderly office was surreal.

She tipped her head down as her hands went to the side closure of her petal-pink wrap blouse.

"No, keep your eyes on me."

Another tilt of her head and she locked eyes with him. By touch, she found the bow on the side and undid the short zipper underneath. She spread the sides wide, revealing her brand-new, blush-colored pushup bra.

"Beautiful, but I want your breasts bare. Lower the cups."

With both hands, she tugged down the satin and lace until her breasts sprang free. The tightness of the material below her full curves plumped them up into high, full mounds as they overflowed the top of her bra. Her nipples constricted, forming hard points, not from the coolness of the room rather from the heat of his avid gaze.

"Your nipples are a lovely rosy pink. They're also very hard. Do they ache?"

"Yes, master. They ache for your touch."

"Pinch them."

Between the tips of her fingers and thumbs, she latched on and squeezed.

"Harder. Do it like I did."

Obediently, she compressed the peaks until the bite of pain made her gasp.

"Good girl. Now, raise your skirt high and spread those lovely thighs nice and wide." The hem was already at her hips, so she tugged it over her behind and moved her thighs apart another inch.

A moment later, he made it clear it wasn't enough. "Wider," he ordered.

This time, she rucked it up all the way to her waist, exposing her bare, uh... She couldn't think the naughty word he'd used but spread as wide as she could go without toppling over.

"Very nice. Reach back and grasp your ankles."

Arched and vulnerable to him, she held her breath as Joseph crouched in front of her.

"Were you a good pet while I was away? Or did you give in to temptation and dip your disobedient subbie fingers into your honey pot as soon as I was out of sight?"

"I was a good girl, master."

He reached out and ran his hand softly down her cheek. Moving to her mouth, he stroked her lower lip with his long middle finger.

"Suck it. Make it nice and wet."

Imagining where that finger would go next, it was all she could do to keep from jumping him and begging him to take her now. But that would never do and would most likely earn her more sexually frustrated waiting. Her lips closed around his long broad finger, and she sucked as bidden, her tongue swirling round and round as she made it wet.

He pulled out with a little pop, which surprised her. No more so than when he lowered his hand to her nipple and ringed it slowly, transferring the wetness.

"This is how I want you when I tell you to kneel. I'm strict with my rules, Olivia. Just like here at work. If you are disobedient, I'll punish you. However, when you obey, I'll reward you with more pleasure than you've ever dreamed of. Can you handle that? Is that what you want?"

"God, yes!"

His fingers tweaked her nipple firmly at her error. "What was that?"

"God, yes, Master Joseph, that's what I want."

He chuckled. "Close enough."

His hand found her bare pussy. "Ah, you're bare and soaking wet. Such a good girl for remembering. It's funny, our brains sometimes get us in trouble, for whatever reason trying to control our reactions, telling our lips to lie or attempting to hide our emotions behind a false persona or mask, but some involuntary responses are beyond its control. Take sexual excitement, for example: flushed cheeks, accelerated breathing, hard nipples, a pussy drenched with honey. All involuntary, thank goodness, making it so our bodies can't lie." His fingers slid through her wetness, pressing more firmly when they reached her clit and circling it slowly, all the while watching her intently.

"Are you hungry, baby?"

"Starving, master."

He chuckled again. "You're beautiful in your submission. You're also very obedient. This pleases me. I believe I mentioned a reward for good behavior. Would you like that now?"

"Yes, please."

"Come to the couch."

She got up and followed him as he walked away, but over his shoulder, he corrected her assumption. "No, pet, I want you to crawl."

She sucked in a shocked breath. No one had asked that of her—ever.

But she wanted to submit, and that meant obeying. She also wanted pleasure beyond her dreams, as he'd promised. After the last twenty-four hours when her body had been rife with need, wanting him and desperately craving release, she wanted that more than anything.

Resigning herself to a new level of submission, she crawled on her hands and knees to where he sat in the middle of his large tufted tweed—yes, tweed—couch.

As she moved toward him, he shrugged out of his jacket and stripped off his tie. Despite her undignified position, Livia felt empowered, her body undulating as she crept slowly forward beneath his unwavering, hungry gaze. She suppressed a grin as he tossed his immaculate clothing heedlessly toward the armrest. Her usually fastidious boss, paying no attention as they fell haphazardly to the floor.

Settling back, he spread his legs, patting his thighs.

She crawled right between them and up into his lap, rubbing against the hard bulge in his trousers as she did so. His hands moved her along by gripping handfuls of her voluptuous ass and guiding her until she straddled him. Joseph's head fell back against the couch as he looked up at her.

"Kiss me," he demanded.

She didn't hesitate to comply with this order, lowering her mouth to his as her fingers sank into his thick, silky hair. When their lips touched, their passions ignited like a match to tinder. Tongues entwined, hands and fingers explored while hips thrust and ground together. It didn't go on long.

In a raspy voice, Joseph ordered, "Raise up. I need to have you now." Sheathed in latex the next instant, he drove upward as he pulled her down, embedding himself deeply and fully. With a cheek in each hand, he ordered, "Ride me, pet."

Her head fell back as she moved over him. Testing the position at first, she eased up and slid back down. His fingers curling into her ass cheeks urged her faster. With his hands as a guide, she picked up the pace, quickly falling into a rhythm.

"That's it," his deep voice hummed in approval. "Fuck yourself with your master's cock."

Like a dual-action piston in a well-oiled machine, they rode each other hard, her body plunging to meet his upward thrusts as they slammed together in a rough, greedy fuck. There was no better way to describe it.

Two days' worth of sexual frustration made Livia's control razor thin. When his hot mouth latched onto a nipple and drew on it fiercely, it was all she could take. Her release, coming after what seemed like an eternity of waiting, emanated from way down in her toes, surging upward until her breathless, ecstatic cries filled the room.

As if waiting for her cue, Joseph's arms tightened, and he flipped her onto her back. Rising over her, he pushed her knees to her chest and came into her harder, driving profoundly deep until he, too, exploded in release. Unlike her airy moans, he came with rough, animalistic groans of satisfaction.

In the aftermath, they cuddled close, Joseph having rolled them to their sides to keep from crushing her. Neither spoke until their bodies eased back to normal from their heightened state.

"Joseph, um...sir, I mean, master?"

He laughed, kissing the tip of her nose. "Joseph is fine now."

"Were you testing me by making me crawl to you?"

"I may have been pushing a bit. Mostly, I wanted to watch your breasts and round ass swaying from side to side while you slinked across the floor. As expected, it was supremely enjoyable."

"How could you see my bottom when you were in front of me?"

He glanced over her shoulder and grinned. "There are at least fifty mirrors on the wall behind you, Livia."

She twisted her head. Her eyes fell on the one-of-a-kind bronze wall sculpture, which was a collection of small mirrors in various shapes and sizes that the artist had rendered in the form of a fish. It had hung there the entire time she'd worked for him.

"Great, just what I've always wanted, my big butt reflected in all its glory on a priceless piece of wall art."

A broad hand landed on her upraised cheek with a resounding smack. Then he grabbed her still tender behind in his broad hands and squeezed, pulling her hips into his.

"This ass is a priceless work of art, and I won't have you denigrating it. That monstrosity"—he jerked his chin toward the fish on the wall—"along with its ridiculous price tag, has always annoyed me."

He studied the piece as he massaged and separated the globes. It took a moment for her to realize he was watching the reflection of his hands working her ass. A rush of heat bathed her cheeks, both upper and lower.

"Now that I look at it in depth, taking in all the subtle shapes, curves, colors, and nuances, I have to admit"—he nudged forward, the hard length of him unmistakable—"it's growing on me."

His eyes dipped to her face. What he found there, which she knew could only be a five-alarm blaze of fiery-cheeked embarrassment, made him grin.

"Still shy even after all I've done to you?" He swatted her behind, playfully light this time. "Get up. I'm taking you home to work on that bashfulness."

While she straightened her hopelessly wrinkled blouse and linen skirt, she felt his eyes on her. Looking up, she caught him with a tender look. Then he winked, something she never expected.

As her mouth gaped open—a response happening more and more around him lately—he laughed.

"Enjoy being clothed while you can, pet. Once I have you naked under my roof, I'm keeping you that way."

Chapter 8

TRUE TO HIS WORD, JOSEPH kept her naked, without so much as a stitch on, for nearly the entire weekend. Helping her overcome her shyness around him was his rationale—not that he needed one—but she suspected it was more because he was enjoying the view as well as free access whenever she was within arm's reach. Neither of which she minded because his touches led to caresses, which progressed to kisses and them getting busy on the nearest flat surface.

Unless they were having sex, he remained fully clothed in contrast to her nudity, which swung the pendulum of power even farther to his side, where it stayed. Even at home, he didn't slouch on his appearance. No ratty T-shirts and sports shorts for this man. Although he eschewed the suit for casual days, he still wore neatly pressed trousers and a button-up shirt.

She teased him about being the only man in Texas that didn't own a pair of jeans, cowboy boots, and a Stetson. But he'd surprised her on Sunday by wearing exactly that when he took her out to brunch. When she laughed with delight at her sexy, swaggering, slightly nerdy cowboy, brunch had almost turned to lunch because Joseph had promptly unzipped his jeans and folded her over the back of the couch for a quickie.

When they came, she wasn't sure if it was only her, or both of them, that shouted *yeehaa*!

Granting her a reprieve from the all-nude weekend, he still limited her attire for brunch to a sundress and sandals, nothing else. This fell under Joseph's newly implemented no-panties-with-dresses rule.

"Are there going to be a lot of them?" she asked as she surrendered her lace bikini panties—that were so skimpy they really shouldn't count—on the way to his car.

"A lot of what?" he asked, grinning, as he tucked them into his jeans pocket.

"Rules," she replied.

He eyed her, one dark brow raised as if to say, *you work for me and you have to ask?*

She remembered typing the revised employee handbook that filled a three-inch binder. Livia added one just like it to her mental shopping list so she could keep up with them all.

As he handed into the car, like a gentleman, she asked, "Why no panties? It's not like we can do anything in the middle of a crowded restaurant."

His grinning response, "You'd be surprised," concerned her. But then he elaborated. "Being bare will be a reminder of my dominance over you, not to mention it will keep you wet and hungry and ready—just how I like you."

The heated glance he gave her, even though it had been only minutes since their quickie, had her squirming in her seat.

Being naked at home with him or under her dress in public made her aware of her body and her proximity to his. She soon caught on to his plan of using texture and touches to push her to the very limits of her control. Like when he brushed by her in the kitchen, allowing the coarseness of his trousers to abrade her bare behind. Or, when he pulled her close for a hug or a kiss ensuring that her hard nipples—which had been in a state of near perpetual stimulation since he'd left her naked and wanting in her apartment—rubbed the placket of his shirt or caught on a button.

Even the few times he allowed her to dress, he'd used subtle touches to keep her aroused. While out for breakfast, while they walked to their table, his hand rode her lower back, but two of his fingers dipped to her behind and rubbed the material of her dress over her pantyless cheeks. Even when they snuggled on the couch while reading the paper or watching the news, he'd curled her into his side such that his shirtsleeve rubbed across her nipples every time he moved.

It was driving her mad. Fortunately, he took her often, relieving the edgy buildup. The only times that she was ill at ease all weekend was when he dragged her down to sit perched on his thigh, a position he seemed to favor but left her uncomfortably aware of the press of her drenched pussy against his pants. When he permitted her to get up, she did so, praying she hadn't left an embarrassing wet spot.

She also learned he was extremely visual, and she often found him watching her. He'd admitted to enjoying the sway of her breasts as she moved, admiring the tempting curves of her hips, and what he called her "exquisitely formed ass."

Joseph wanted her close, touching her near constantly when they were in the same room. He ordered her closer with a soft, "come here, pet," whenever she wandered too far away.

If occupied with a task, he delighted in posing her provocatively. While preparing their lunch on Saturday—that he cooked was something else new she learned about him—he picked her up and plopped her bare bottom on the cold granite counter. He positioned her like a mud flap pinup, leaning back on her hands, breasts uplifted, and legs spread with her heels to her ass, leaving her pussy on blatant display. He'd sliced fresh fruit, playfully placing slices of strawberry on her nipples and kiwi low on her belly. As their omelet was cooking, he'd nibbled each piece off, licking her belly and lingering over her aching tips long after any residue of flavor could have lingered.

Later that day, while he was taking a phone call in his office, he had her on his lap at his desk. Facing him, with her feet flat on the armrests, legs splayed wide apart, he pushed her head back until it was resting on his desktop. Then the evil man had put the phone on speaker and played with her—fingers and mouth teasing her hard nipples and playing with her clit—while she bit her tongue and tried desperately to hold back her moans. He'd told her to be prepared to surrender if she came to him and he hadn't been joking.

As much great sex as they had, they were also incredibly intimate on a nonsexual level, snuggling and holding each other close as they talked. At one point, she asked Joseph something she'd always wondered. They were lying on the couch in the aftermath of Joseph taking her against the living room wall. Brought on by the simple act of Livia walking across the room, he'd lifted her until their hips aligned, then with her legs around his waist and her back to the wall, he'd taken her. It was carnal, spontaneous, and utterly amazing.

Afterward, lying on the plush area rug in his living room, relaxed in one another's arms, she blurted out, "Why didn't you ever marry?"

Silence followed.

"If you want to tell me, I mean," she rushed to say. "I shouldn't have asked. I'm sorry."

The arm wrapped around her waist gave her a firm squeeze. "Hush, baby. I've got nothing to hide. I was married once, a long time ago."

She rose on an elbow and gazed down at him. "I don't think anyone knows that at work."

"The office gossip mill must be on the fritz. Have you heard any other good dirt about me?"

"It can't be very accurate. No one knows you're a dom."

"I should hope not." He reached up and tucked several strands of loose blonde hair coiled on his chest behind her ear. "Not that I'm ashamed of what I am, but I prefer keeping my private life private. That's why I play at the club."

"Because it's two hours away," she said, nodding. She'd done the same thing.

"That and because they thoroughly screen their members. And guests have to come by recommendation of a member, or they don't get in."

"I didn't," she replied, although she had to fill out a bunch of paperwork.

"You just wandered in off the street?" he challenged.

"Well, no. I had an invitation that was arranged by a friend of a friend."

"One or both of whom vouched for you."

"Ah..."

"You also had to sign an ironclad confidentiality agreement which, if broken could be financially painful. I know because

I wrote it." He tapped her nose with his finger. "And you, my pretty pet, typed it for me."

"I did?"

"Yep. About two years ago. It may have seemed generic, but believe me, it wasn't."

She shifted, stacked her fists on his chest and her chin on top of them. "What happened that your marriage didn't work out?"

"It was right out of law school. We were both focused on our careers more than each other and definitely didn't jive in the bedroom. She was strictly vanilla."

"Why on earth did you marry her?"

"Ella and I were friends, classmates, and lovers, but we were never in love. It was a huge mistake. At twenty-five, I didn't know who I was or what I wanted other than my career. That came through loud and clear in a relationship. After the divorce, a friend of mine introduced me to the club scene. Dominance and submission felt instantly right to me and filled a void that previous relationships had not. After that, vanilla was a flavor I no longer enjoyed."

"That was nearly twenty years ago. Did you give up on marriage after that?"

"Not necessarily. I was open to it if I found the right woman. You know as well as I how difficult that can be in the lifestyle."

She did. She'd crashed and burned too many times.

"Do you regret not having children?"

"Not with Ella. It was a clean break. Children would have made it extremely messy."

She frowned. Not liking the sound of that at all.

Well attuned to her moods, even after such a short time, Joseph shifted and toppled her onto her back. Then, propped on a forearm, he leaned over her, cupping her cheek in his free hand.

"If you're trying to find out if I'm anti-marriage and anti-kids, I'm not. Although this weekend has proven we have something very promising growing here, three days might be a bit early to write vows and hire a decorator for the nursery."

She balked. "Oh no, I didn't mean—"

"I know you didn't, pet. With me, marriage and kids are still on the table. So you aren't spinning your wheels. Got it?"

"Yes, sir." She flushed at his ability to read her so easily. "Were you always this perceptive?"

"Hardly," he laughed, shifting so that he was fully on top of her. "I had a beautiful submissive under my nose for years and didn't know it. That's pretty clueless, don't you think?"

"Yeah, for a while there I thought you were gay."

His head, which had lowered to nibble along her bare shoulder, reared back in surprise. "What? Why on earth did you think that?"

"Joseph, if my skirts were any tighter, I would have split a seam. When you didn't notice or ever make a pass, I thought I wasn't your type or gender."

"Damn."

She giggled. "Didn't you wonder why I was always getting things out of a bottom drawer when you were around? I put everything down low on purpose. If you had looked, you would have found all the top ones completely empty."

When he blinked, she could practically see all the times she'd stuck her bottom virtually in his face flash before his eyes.

"You imp," he accused as his fingers danced along her ribs, grinning as she squirmed and laughed beneath his merciless tickling. When she begged him to stop, he did, kissing her hard instead.

After a moment, he raised his head. Pure green sparkled down on her as a hand slipped to her backside and he palmed a cheek.

"I noticed everything about this glorious ass, every shimmy, shake, and definitely every tight little skirt. Believe me." He dipped his head to brush her lips again lightly. "I missed the submissive signs, clearly. In my fantasies, you were the submissive of my dreams, but in reality, you were my efficient, straitlaced, extremely hot secretary who I didn't want to offend with unwanted advances even when she made me rock hard every day."

"They wouldn't have been unwanted."

"I know that now, Livia, but for all that time I was blind." His mouth kicked up on one side in a grin. "Take a memo, Miss Wright. First thing Monday morning, make an appointment with my optometrist. Obviously, I need a stronger prescription."

Chapter 9

THEIR IDYLLIC WEEKEND flew by and reality returned bright and early Monday morning. Nattily dressed in a suit—a lightweight tweed in blue, gray, and brown over-check with co-ordinating blue buttons and solid trousers—jaw clean-shaven and smooth, his hair perfectly combed, Joseph drove her to the office in his Jag. She sat beside him in her usual snug skirt, silk blouse, and four-inch heels. Outwardly, she tried to put on a brave front, but inside, her stomach was twisted in knots.

He pulled into his reserved parking space and switched off the ignition at the same time she released a tremulous sigh.

"Olivia, relax."

"Arriving in the same car and walking in together is as good as taking out a billboard at Fredericksburg Road and the 410 Loop. Everyone will know."

"So what if they do?"

"I can hear the gossip and jokes now. It's the old stereotype about the boss chasing the secretary around his desk. They'll know I was caught and surrendered in the end."

Turning to her with a grin, his finger brushed down her cheek in a now familiar caress. "And in quite spectacular fashion, I must say."

Blushing, she glanced away. "I'll be crucified in the office grapevine, Joseph."

"Perhaps, but it will pass quickly. Someone else will have a more scandalous and juicier tidbit of gossip in a day or two and we'll be forgotten."

"Would it be okay if we keep up the appearance of professionalism while at work?"

He chuckled. "I don't plan to fuck you on your desk with the door wide open, if that's your concern."

"Joseph!" His language, she noted, got rather blunt and quite kitschy when he spoke of sex. Until a few days ago, the worst she'd ever heard him utter was damn.

He leaned in to brush her lips with a kiss, undeterred when she turned her head at the last moment. Instead, he whispered teasingly in her ear, "How about I reserve all fucking for my office behind the locked door? Will that do?"

Even if this wasn't the 1950s or the set of *Mad Men*, where a little office slap and tickle or being bent over the boss's desk was the norm, women still took the hit in the reputation column with an office affair. She was serious, and he was being flippant. It stung and to cover the mist of tears that threatened to become a deluge, she looked away.

His fingers caught her chin and turned her face back to his, sobering when he took in her distress.

"Aw, pet, I'm sorry. You have valid concerns about this, and I'm being crass." His other hand came up and with both thumbs, he wiped away the few tears that had already escaped. "We'll keep things aboveboard at the office if that's what you want. And, despite my off-color humor just now, I have no intention of flaunting it or embarrassing you. I'm not hiding our relationship, however, just the intimate details. If I want to have lunch with you or take you to a cocktail party as my date, I will. They're used to seeing us together. Soon, they'll be used to us as a couple. You can trust me on this. And, I promise, if there is the first hint of nastiness, I'll nip it in the bud."

Her hand rose to his cheek. That he thought he had power over titillating gossip and the office rumor mill was naïve but sweet. "I do trust you, Joseph. Thank you."

His lips brushed hers softly. "We better go, or we'll be late. You know how the boss is about punctuality."

She grinned when he winked. As he walked around to open her door, images of being called on the carpet by Mr. Hooks and being taken to task over his desk filled her oversexed mind.

THE WEEK FLEW BY. WITH a huge class action filing imminent, the firm was busy, and it was all hands on deck preparing the documents. Joseph's schedule was hectic with court three days, new client interviews, and an impromptu return to Ft. Worth for another deposition on Thursday. She'd been in his bed for five straight nights, but on Wednesday went home alone. By the close of business the following day, she was missing him terribly.

To make matters worse, his return flight was delayed. When he walked in after lunch, giving her only a discreet peck on the cheek in greeting, she regretted her request for professionalism in the office.

The adage *be careful what you ask for* rattled around in her head, not stopping when Joseph came out of his office an hour later on his way to court.

"Do you have those two motions for me to look over?" he asked as he strode out, his briefcase in one hand while he straightened his tie with the other. A black-and-white pin-dot bow tie to be exact, which contrasted perfectly with another lightweight tweed suit, in dark gray. He was the only man she knew who wore a bow tie, but as sexy as Joseph was, he worked it.

Distracted by his glittering green-eyed gaze and warm smile, she handed him the folder with the documents. Her vision became hazy with longing when he ran his thumb over the apple of her cheek in thanks. As her eyes followed him to the door, she noticed the long square box on the console table.

"I almost forgot. That package came for you earlier." She motioned toward it when he glanced back. Stopping briefly, he eyed the label while saying nothing, but there was a sparkle of excitement illuminating his gaze that hadn't been there before when he glanced her way again.

"Get us a table at the Fig Tree tonight," he said quietly. "My mouth is watering for Sea Scallops."

"Sounds wonderful," she replied, thinking a kiss and them getting naked on the couch in his office sounded a million times better than the city's best seafood.

"Make it for six o'clock. We'll be home by nine for dessert. I missed you, pet, so be warned. You are the only sweet course I have in mind." With a wink, he was gone.

Warmth spread through her and her fantasies were on the lustful side as she stood staring longingly at the empty doorway for some time. With a deep sigh, she forced herself to get back to work.

Taking her seat, her eyes scanned the files scattered across the surface of her desk. That's when it hit her. Frantically, she rifled through several folders then pulled out drawers and sifted through the file folders there as well. When she found the one she was looking for, she opened it and scanned the documents. Then she groaned, dropping her head on her desk with a thud.

Feeling lonely yesterday, she'd had a fleeting idea. It was childish really, so she'd pushed it aside and gone back to work. But the idea kept returning, along with her recurring fantasy of Joseph spanking her over her desk. Throughout the long day, it kept popping into her head at the oddest times.

Frustrated, she set out to make it a reality. It hadn't taken her over ten minutes to switch the names of two clients on two different contracts. When she was done, she stared down at the documents, the incorrect names patently obvious and practically leaping off the typewritten pages.

She'd thought to force his hand, testing how he would react to such a careless error now that their relationship had changed. Knowing it was a stupid and immature game, she'd abandoned the idea and had meant to shred them, but someone had come in and distracted her. She had no intention of following through with her silly scheme.

Crap! How could she have given him the wrong file?

She picked up the phone and dialed Emma.

"Got time for coffee?" she asked without a greeting when her best friend answered on the first ring. "I've screwed up bigtime and need some advice on how to mitigate the damage."

ENTERING HIS CLIENT'S not guilty plea didn't take more than a few minutes and despite the busy time of day, the trip to the courthouse and back took under an hour. This placed him back in the office before two o'clock.

Livia's desk was conspicuously empty when he returned. With a pile of work waiting for him, he got right to it, leaving his door open. A few minutes passed before he heard her in the outer office.

"Olivia, come in here, please." He didn't have to raise his voice or call twice, hearing her chair roll across the floor as soon as he'd asked for her. When she appeared in the doorway, he added, "Bring the package with you."

Through the open doorway, he saw her cross the room, losing sight of her for a moment as she retrieved the box. Only a few seconds ticked by until she reappeared, stepping into his office almost hesitantly, the long box in hand. He refrained from grinning, just barely, at his little imp.

She knew exactly what he wanted. As if he would miss such an obvious blunder. He didn't do probate law, but the junior associates he supervised did. The documents were for their cases. If they'd slipped by him with errors, both he and Livia would have been embarrassed. He'd been irritated at first that she would make such a careless mistake, which wasn't like her. Then he realized her game.

"Come in and shut the door." Once she pulled the door closed, he ordered, "Lock it, please."

He saw her stiffen and a moment later, the soft snick of the lock echoed in the quiet room. With her back to him, he heard her take a slow, steadying breath before she turned to face him.

When she approached, he stopped her.

"Stay right there."

She halted mid-stride then moved back. Her hands clasped the box in a white-knuckled grip he expected to crush the cardboard any minute. She fidgeted slightly, shifting her weight restlessly from side to side as she waited. The picture of a naughty child caught with her hand in the cookie jar.

"The documents you gave me earlier were unacceptable. Imagine if Sister Ernestine at St. Lady of Benedict's got Mr. Armenture's will, leaving all his worldly possessions, not to his wife but his three mistresses instead."

She blanched. He wondered if she just now caught the irony of her gaffe.

"Do you have anything to say for yourself? This sloppiness is quite unlike you."

"I'm terribly sorry, sir. I'll have the corrected contracts for you in a jiffy."

He stood and walked around to the front of his desk. Perching on the edge, he leaned back, crossing his ankles in a laid-back manner. "You seem tense. Is there something you aren't telling me?"

As he waited for her answer, he removed a cloth from his jacket pocket and cleaned his glasses, nonchalant and as though he were unperturbed.

"Only that I'm very sorry for my carelessness and it won't happen again."

"Open the package for me. It's a special order, one I hadn't expected to need so soon, but it seems it will come in handy today."

She peeled off the packing tape and opened the flap. Looking inside, her face went pale and her eyes shot to him.

"Remove the contents, please, and bring it here. I'll need to inspect each item before I use it on one of my most valued possessions."

Backhanded praise, if he'd ever heard it. She frowned, as he knew she would.

"Come along, pet. Don't add procrastination to your list of misdeeds today."

She removed the items he'd selected expressly with Livia in mind. The first was a riding crop with a wide leather keeper on the end. She gave it a cursory glance obviously having seen one before.

He held out his hand. "I'll take that. What else do we have?"

Her brows gathered fiercely as she withdrew the Dragon cane. Denser than rattan, with greater flexibility, it was less likely to fracture during use. It also had a handle, which made for a better grip and less slippage, which could lead to injury. The idea of an unintentional mark on her fine ass was unthinkable. Palm outstretched, he silently asked for the cane as well.

"There should be one more item."

"What in the world?" she whispered as she held up the Broom Brush, which was a modern-day birching rod.

He relieved her of the implement and the box, setting the latter on the floor out of his way.

"I'll explain while you strip."

He noted the muscles in her throat contract as she swallowed, and her fingers trembled ever so slightly as she worked the buttons on her blouse.

"The brush, sweet Livia, is a modern-day tool inspired by the Victorian era birch rod. In 1870, had you made such an egregious error, I would have collected a bundle of switches and whacked away at your naughty bottom." He shook his head, making a tsking sound. "Imagine how messy that was with the bark and broken bits flying all about as the master flailed the inattentiveness out of his charge."

Her eyes practically bugged out, clearly thinking of her thrashed behind, not a mess on the floor. In her very expressive face, he could easily read every nuance of her dismay, along with a healthy dose of curiosity and excitement. Although he planned to use it on her forthwith, he upped the psychological ante with the drawn-out explanation. A hard lesson to be sure, but the imp deserved it for her little prank, by god. He bit the inside of his cheek, trying to keep his amusement under control.

"This beauty"—he continued, watching with undisguised interest as she slipped off her bra—"is made of rattan, scaled down and painstakingly polished into these smooth reeds. That was another drawback of the old birch rods, rough edges, and knots in the wood. This is flawless. Don't get me wrong. It is a severe implement and in the wrong hands can raise welts and break the skin, but in the control of a skilled master, it can range from pleasurable wispy strokes to stinging fire, as is its reputation. If punishment is the goal, added strokes and a bit more effort can make this highly effective in correcting recalcitrant subordinates."

She had removed her skirt. No panties, he noticed, pleased she had followed his new rule. This left her in a lacy champagne-colored garter and sheer stockings. His already stiff cock jerked at the lovely sight. She'd been planning a welcome home for him, apparently.

"Leave the rest and bend over my desk."

As she took her position, he saw the slight tremble in her shoulders and the rapid thrum of her pulse in her throat. If he touched her now, he knew she'd be dripping wet.

With a touch intending to soothe, he softly glided his hand down her spine. A little anxiety was good, but he didn't want her frightened. It was play, not torture, although she didn't know that yet. Having easily taken control of the game, he wondered if it was turning out as she'd hoped.

His fingers skimmed along her lower back and into the waistband of the garter. "Palms flat on the surface, feet wide apart." As she shifted, his hand moved between her legs and commanded, "Wider."

Her breath hitched as his fingers found her sultry heat. She was soaked, her abundant nectar like a balm to his soul. His Livia thrived on this as much as he did, thank god. In that, they were a perfect match.

Returning his hand to her back for support, he whisked the birch broom lightly across both cheeks of her nicely rounded ass.

"I'm told there is a cumulative effect with the birch. Each swat builds upon the next." He paused, delivering one well-controlled *thwack* after another. She shifted a bit. "I'm assured builds to a significant sting." He paused and rubbed his palm on her pinkening skin, assessing the heat. Deciding she could take more, he administered a half dozen consecutive swipes, each equal to if not eclipsing its predecessor.

On the last stroke, she hissed in a quickly indrawn breath.

He stopped, his hand gliding over her quivering ass as he leaned over her back. "If you want to play naughty secretary and me your hard-ass, disciplinarian boss, pet, you only need to say so."

She huffed a sharp breath at both his words and the two fingers that simultaneously slid into her wet pussy. Finding her clit with his thumb, he rubbed it briskly as he pumped in and out of her slickness.

"I'll make the time. If you want to role-play, I'm up for that, too, but none of this sham incompetence. I know you better."

"I'm sorry," she said between moans. "I didn't mean—"

She didn't speak further, or perhaps, she couldn't, as he withdrew one finger and slipped it into her wonderfully tight and puckered rear hole.

"Go on," he encouraged as his fingers moved in and out of both holes in tandem, his thumb strumming constantly over the bundle of nerves up front.

"I can't think when you're doing that."

"Try," he insisted.

"The f-folder..." she stammered as he quickened the pace. "I didn't intend to give it to you," she blurted out in a rush. "I mean, I did, at first. Then I changed my mind. The original contracts are on my desk."

"You were going to give me a little test, eh? Were you hoping I'd bend you over my desk for a sound thrashing?"

Her answer, "yes, master," was almost lost in the bliss-filled moan that escaped from her throat as she rocked back against his persistent hand.

"It seems a spanking in this case is a reward rather than a punishment when that was your end game all along."

He withdrew his hand, smiling as she whimpered at its loss. He didn't plan to leave her wanting for long, however.

From his trouser pocket, he withdrew the plug and lube he'd placed there in anticipation of this moment. One-handed, he thumbed open the flip-top bottle and applied several drops to the end of the medium-sized plug. He gently spread her cheeks and pressed the tip against the small opening his finger had primed.

"You've taken a plug before, haven't you, pet?"

"Yes, sir. A small one, but it has been years."

It could have been decades. That some other dom had plugged her ass infuriated him. He knew his anger was irrational. Any woman who'd reached her thirties, submissive or vanilla, would have a sexual past. He just preferred not to think of it, but as her dom, he had to know when introducing new things.

"Breathe out while you bear down, and it will slide right in."

Slowly, he inserted the plug, watching as her ass stretched to accommodate its girth before eagerly engulfing it. He had to wrap his arm around her waist to hold her still while he seated it fully.

"The end has a pink jewel which looks lovely peeking out between your birched cheeks," he murmured, bending to place a gentle kiss on each side. A few more with the birch on her plugged behind then he'd grant her clemency and fuck her.

He resumed with the same intensity as if he hadn't ceased; swishing the rod along the fullness of her backside, further heating her skin, and bringing it from pale to rosy pink.

"Please, master, I can't bear it. May I come?"

"Not without me inside you. You'll have to wait."

He moved to her thighs and, as he painted them pink with the brush, he opened his zipper with his spare hand. Unleashed, his painfully distended cock jerked in his palm at the sound of her unrestrained cries, and he almost erupted prematurely.

With an urgency matching her own, he slicked the head through her drenched folds then changed angles and filled her swiftly. The plug in her ass made the squeeze even tighter. He thrust hard, wedging himself deep, sweat beading up on his forehead as he fought for control.

She was at the edge, however. "Please...master," she sobbed.

"Come, Livia. Fly apart for me."

She did, screaming her pleasure, uncaring who might overhear. Knowing that she would after their passion had receded, he slipped his hand over her mouth, muffling her cries. His roar of completion followed shortly and was only incrementally less noisy even when he buried his face in the side of her neck.

When he lifted his chest from her back and pulled out, he whispered in her ear, "Stay right here."

Joseph disappeared into his private lavatory, returning in a moment with a warm cloth and cleansed her gently. When he was done, he helped her stand and hugged her against him.

"Get dressed, pet. When you're done, bring me the correct contracts. One needs to go out by courier by close of business today."

She nodded and took a step. Halting sharply, her hands flew to her bottom, and she swung back. "You forgot the plug."

"No, I didn't," he countered, bending to place a quick kiss on her lips. "That is your punishment for testing me."

"But I didn't. What I did today was an actual mistake."

"Which wouldn't have happened without your scheming. The plug which you'll wear until I say it comes out will help you remember the next time you think plotting against your master might be fun."

He patted her behind, tapping the plug with his fingertips. Her little squeal and shudder told him she wasn't much above a novice with ass play. She would find out soon enough that the plug would shift with every subtle movement and if she sat or heaven forbid bent over—

At that point, she did exactly that, leaning down to retrieve her skirt from the floor. She yelped, popping upright instantly. Her grimace soon turned into a scowl, which she indiscreetly aimed his way.

His good humor boosted his tolerance level, not to mention he'd just come inside her. So he let her off easy with a warning.

"Without the scowl please, pet. Unless you want to try out our new cane. I promise it will be less forgiving than the birch, as will I."

"No, master. I'm fresh out of scowls."

When she finished dressing, he beckoned her over with a crooked finger. As soon as she came within reach, he hooked his hand around her nape and pulled her into him, bending to capture her lips in a scorching kiss. Once he had her breathless, he reluctantly let her go.

"I enjoyed our little interlude. Maybe we should renegotiate professional behavior in the office."

"After the last hour, I think we already have."

He grinned. "Cheeky girl, I believe you're right."

She returned his grin, standing on tiptoes for one more quick kiss. Of course, he obliged. As she walked away, her gait was noticeably less graceful and polished. He couldn't help the chuckle that earned him a glare as she opened the door.

"Was that a scowl, Miss Wright?"

"No, Mr. Hooks," she replied without looking back. "Something in my eye, is all," was her unlikely excuse. Before she slipped out of sight, she winked at him brazenly.

His laughter rolled up and burst free. She was a delight, and he kicked himself for not making a move with her sooner. For the rest of the afternoon, he enjoyed watching her try to manage the plug, challenging her by sending her on needless errands, calling her into his office a time or two for a kiss or a pat, and once bending her over on the outrageous excuse of checking the placement of the plug.

By five o'clock, she'd had enough. Without warning, she rushed into his office, locked the door, and sank to her knees.

"Please, master, end this torment and fuck me."

Seeing her in such a state, his simmering passion boiled over. He got up without a word, grabbed her hand as he passed, and with her doubled over the arm of the couch, he replaced the plug with his cock.

Going slow at first, he wrapped his arm around her hips, his hand dipping between her thighs to torment her clit. She was soon begging for more. Only then did he speed up, taking her hard and fast.

It occurred to him, after they'd both shouted in release, it might be a good idea to get a few estimates on soundproofing his office.

Chapter 10

WITH LIVIA PRACTICALLY living with Joseph, spending every night at his place unless he was out of town, Emma and David insisted on meeting him.

"I know Emma from the office," he said, as he navigated evening traffic on the way to her friends' house for dinner. "I've never met her husband, however. Give me the run down on your history so I know what to expect."

"I met David at a munch I attended in college. It was my first, and we chatted. He was full of information and took me under his wing, not as a submissive but more as a mentor. We were instant friends, having no kind of romantic or sexual spark." She glanced over at Joseph, who was listening to her ramble as he drove. "We adopted each other, I'm afraid. Neither of us has any siblings, but he couldn't be more of a brother to me if he tried. I hope you understand."

"I'm glad he was there for you, Livia. What about Emma? Was she ever jealous of your connection?"

"Never. She sees the brother/sister connection we have. He left town to complete his doctoral degree back east, which is where he met Emma. The two of them couldn't be more perfect for one another."

That had been a difficult two years for her. During his absence, without David's support and sound advice to keep her straight, she'd gotten mixed up with Vaughn. She hadn't disclosed anything about him just yet and wondered if she should.

Glancing out the window, she reflected on their unhealthy relationship. It was nothing like what she and Joseph shared. He could be strict, but mostly he was affectionate and playful. She'd laughed more in her short time with Joseph than she had the entire time she was with Vaughn who was his complete opposite—overbearing, demeaning, and frankly an ass.

When they'd returned from Dallas, Emma and David had immediately recognized the relationship as toxic and challenged her on it, but she'd been in denial. Vaughn had kept her apart from them after that. She was a shell of herself while with him, something he seemed to prefer.

Once she'd become entirely dependent on him and isolated from her support system, he'd broken things off, leaving her devastated. He was a ginormous prick, but it had taken a while for her to see the truth and realize that dumping her was the best thing Vaughn had ever done for her.

"Livia?"

Startled out of her musings, she looked away from the window.

"Where did you go just now? You were so far away you didn't hear me call you twice."

"Lost in the past for a bit, is all." That wasn't a lie, not completely, more like a half-truth. She pressed on. "You asked about Emma. We clicked right off. I was involved with someone at the time, and she never saw me as a threat. Now my brother's wife is my best friend."

"Meaning, I should be prepared for the Inquisition from them both?"

"It won't be as bad as that. David's a tough dom, but he only tops Emma now. Ten years ago, he may very well have put you on his rack to get the truth out of you. Muah, ha ha ha." She giggled, her earlier somberness dispelled. "Truly, though, they're my only family. They love me and want to see me happy. I think once they meet you, they'll love you as much as I do."

Realizing immediately that she'd let the L-word slip out, she cringed inwardly, waiting stiffly for a response. Holy crap! Had she screwed up and let it out too soon? It had only been a month.

"Livia," he said softly, his hand finding hers and lifting it to his lips. After a gentle brush, he held it clenched on his hard thigh. "Although a declaration while driving wasn't my intention, since it's out there...I love you, too. If you're worried that it's too fast, consider that although we've only been a couple, and dom and sub for a few short weeks, we've known one another for much longer, and the feelings were there well before that night at Club Decadence. Don't you agree?"

"Yes," she whispered, squeezing his hand. "I've loved you forever, it seems."

He grinned at her obvious exaggeration but didn't discount her fervent declaration. "I'd prefer you turn that around a bit."

She thought for a moment and restated her feelings. "I will love you forever, Joseph."

He brought her hand to his lips once again. "That is indeed sweet music to my ears, love."

THE EVENING WITH HER friends wasn't awkward as she feared. Instead, it was filled with delicious food, great company, a lot of wine, and plenty of laughter. Joseph and David hit it off right away, both having so much in common. The only uncomfortable moment came during after-dinner coffee. She had snuggled up next to Joseph on the love seat while their hosts shared the oversized chair-and-a-half, petite Emma ensconced in David's lap. Somehow, the conversation turned to Livia's extremely poor taste in men.

"Hopefully, Joseph, you can help her break the pattern." David went on half-jokingly, "Of course, if it's her heart that gets broken, I'll be obligated to lop off a certain appendage, which is what I should have done with that bastard Vaughn."

Her dom stiffened beside her, his full attention shifting to her. She directed her frown at David for making things awkward, which was also a good way of avoiding looking at Joseph directly.

"I don't believe she's mentioned anything about 'Vaughn the bastard,' have you, Olivia?"

"We haven't discussed past relationships at all, not in detail."

She felt the heat of his gaze but resisted meeting it. She really didn't want to get into this now—or ever. The wine had put David in a talkative mood, and much to her detriment, he warmed to the topic of her evil ex.

"Vaughn Steros was an abusive prick," David supplied, turning a dark glower on Livia. "And you, missy, should know better than withholding something so pivotal in your past from your dom."

Two on one, so not fair. She looked to Emma for help, but she was frowning at her, too. Definitely outnumbered and out-gunned. She shifted to get up, but Joseph's arms tightened.

"It was a long time ago. Can't we move on?"

"The better question," David quipped, "is, have you?"

"How can you ask that when I'm sitting beside..." Her hand waved over Joseph's long frame, which would dwarf Vaughn's by almost a foot.

"She's got you there, babe," Emma drawled. "He is, without a doubt, an upgrade."

"It seems you'll have to fill me in since she clearly doesn't want to share," Joseph stated, his voice which had been warm and relaxed earlier, having taken on a noticeable chill. "Was the abuse physical?"

"No," Livia interjected, but got a silencing squeeze. Joseph had moved on to another more reliable witness, evidently. She glanced down at her clasped hands, really not wanting to get into this.

"There were never any visible bruises, but his words hurt as much as a fist. He beat her up emotionally," Emma explained, reaching out to squeeze her friend's hand. "After he stripped her bare and left her defenseless, the bastard dumped her when she turned thirty-five like it was a preordained cutoff point. Then, to add insult to injury, he showed up a month later with a col-lege kid on his arm. If she was twenty, I'd be surprised."

"Keep it together, sweetheart," David quietly advised.

"I don't know if I can," Emma said, angry on her behalf. Flicking her hand her way, she exclaimed, "He must be blind because look at her. She's thirty-eight but could pass for twen-ty-eight and is fah-reaking gorgeous. And she will be at forty-eight and sixty-eight. Trust me, I've seen her mother. By my way of thinking, he did her a favor, but it took a while for us to convince her of that."

"Can we change the subject, please?" Livia implored softly.

"Silence, pet."

The endearment was common in the lifestyle, but Joseph had only used it in private. He didn't hesitate in front of Emma and David. They'd understand its meaning, and said in his no-nonsense tone, would recognize he was serious about dredging up the ugliness that Livia clearly didn't want to.

"I blame myself," David's low voice rumbled, his anger rivaling his tiny wife's. "I was away for two years while working on my PhD and completing my internship. She'd talked about him, but whenever I came home for a visit, he was always out of town or he cancelled when a work matter suddenly came up. I suspected something was wrong, but Livia convinced me I was imagining things. Finally, about two years in, I got the chance to meet him. It took about two minutes in his presence to recognize he wasn't a dom but an abusive bully. Trying to persuade her he wasn't good for her wasn't enough. I should have done a helluva a lot more."

"I was an adult, David. What more could you have done? I didn't listen when you tried to warn me. It's not on you, but on me," she ended in a whisper. Drawing on Joseph's strength, she pressed closer against his side. "Not long after the breakup, I transferred into your office. The change was good for me, but it took a while to come back to myself. David and Emma helped me."

"It wasn't just us, Liv," he added gently. "You need to tell him all of it."

Livia glared at him again. Was nothing private with these doms?

Joseph intercepted the look and turned her face up to his. "Don't take this out on him. David knows how important disclosure of past trauma is in our lifestyle, not to mention honesty and trust. By revealing your remarkably imprudent omission, it shows his concern and love for you. You should have told me this first thing, so he didn't have to."

"I know that," she whispered. "It's just so embarrassing."

"To have fallen in love?"

"No. To be pathetic and weak. That's how he made me feel."

"This happened three years ago. Is that why you never got involved again?"

"I was being cautious," she said evasively.

"Olivia," David cut in, repeating, "tell him all of it."

"I was getting to it," she snapped. Immediately, she apologized. "I'm sorry, David. I shouldn't have bitten your head off. It's just that I'd rather forget this ugly chapter in my life."

When she took a deep, steadying breath, his arms curled around her. Pulling her in rather than pushing her away, providing his support, thank goodness, which was unlike what she'd experienced with the only long-term dom in her past.

"I was in a dark place. The doctor called it clinical depression. It took counseling and medication before I felt like myself again." She glanced up at him to see how he was taking it all. Seeing no disapproval or condemnation, she added, "I'm off the antidepressants and my therapy sessions have ended. The change in jobs, David coming home and having him and Emma in my life really helped me heal. There was also this really hot attorney who caught my eye."

Joseph's grunt was the only acknowledgement of her attempt to lighten the mood. "Have you been with anyone since the bastard? Am I the first in three years?"

"I've had a few dates."

"You know that isn't what I meant."

"I did a few scenes at a few clubs and parties, but nothing serious."

"She pushed them away," David put in. "Just like she tried to do to you that first night. Thank god you had the balls to call her on her shit."

Joseph's eyes searched hers while stroking her cheek. Suddenly, they shifted to David. "Knowing all of this, why the hell did you let her go clubbing by herself? What the fuck?"

Shocked at his language, Livia stiffened. She'd never heard Joseph use fuck as an exclamation or expletive. A verb during play, yes, but never in this context. Shock quickly turned to dread, as she realized her other omission from that night was about to come to light.

"I'm getting a headache—"

"Stop being avoidant, Olivia. We're doing this now. Sit there and be quiet unless you have something of value to add. If you can't do so, I'm sure David has a gag I can borrow." He paused, obviously done with her crap. "Are we clear on this?"

"Yes, sir."

His eyes reconnected with David, who was shaking his head, perceptively offended. "I'd never let her go to a club alone. She always went with me and Emma."

"She was at Decadence alone."

Two pairs of eyes turned to her; one set angry, the other appalled.

"I arranged for a colleague, who was also a member, to escort her." David's blue-eyed gaze blazed with fire as his words mirrored Joseph's. "What the fuck, Livia?"

"My escort canceled at the last minute. I was afraid if I didn't go, I wouldn't get another chance."

"How did you walk into that place by yourself?" Emma gasped.

"It wasn't easy, or the smartest thing I've ever done. But if I hadn't gone, things might not have turned out as they did."

"The end doesn't justify the means, little one."

"Was that the only time?" David barked, his face telling her he already knew the answer.

So she didn't. Answer that is, which was as good as admitting the truth.

"Fuck me," he growled. His eyes shot to Joseph. "She's a handful, man. Sweet as hell, but when she gets a bug up her ass—"

"David!" Livia and Emma both cried at once.

"No need to worry," Joseph assured him. "I've had plenty of practice handling a disobedient submissive. More so of late, which Livia can attest to." He stood and tugged her up beside him. "Thank you for dinner and a very informative evening. I think Olivia and I will continue this discussion at home."

"What about dessert?" she asked, sending a wide-eyed look Emma's way as she tried to stall.

"What about your headache?" Joseph challenged.

At the door, he turned. "I almost forgot. I wanted to invite the both of you to join us one night at the club. There are some preliminary forms to fill out and approvals to get beforehand, similar to what Olivia had to go through. But if you're interested in putting in the work, I think you might enjoy the club."

Emma practically flew off David's lap and jumped up and down in her excitement, while his reaction was more sedate. Rising, he clamped an arm around her shoulders, trying to contain her as he graciously accepted on their behalf.

Despite what lay in store for her later, Livia smiled at her friend's exuberance. "You'll like it, Em. There's a great band with an awesome singer and the owners' submissives are all very nice."

"I can't wait to see the dungeon. Maybe this time, you can, too."

Blinking slowly, Livia looking up at Joseph. He smiled warmly, clearly recalling that night as fondly as she did. Needlessly, she stated, "I told her I never made it past the bar."

David's attention switched to Joseph's and back. "I thought you two, you know."

She flushed under David's regard and admitted, "I fainted when I saw him, and he carried me to a room upstairs."

"Have you ever heard anything so romantic, babe?" Emma asked, dreamily.

"It was one of the owners' private apartments," Joseph explained. "We have an arrangement. They let me stay because of the long commute and I represent them as well as all their women when they get into legal trouble. Believe me, they're getting a bargain."

David's eyes once again snapped with anger as they zoned in on Livia. "Let me get this straight. You went to a club alone, picked up a dom, and went directly to his private apartment? Olivia Suzanne, did you retain nothing I taught you?"

"But it was Joseph, David. Besides, I was unconscious, and didn't have much say in what happened."

"Fuck me," he repeated with a groan, his hands raking through his hair in frustration. "Joseph, my man, please give her a few swats for me."

"Not a problem, my friend."

"Hey," Livia protested, stopping her hands—just barely—from flying protectively to her bottom.

"Save your breath, pet. No amount of protests will get you out of your punishment for this." He bid David and Emma goodnight, adding, "I'll be in touch about your visit."

With his hand firmly gripping hers, he headed out. She looked back at her friends beseechingly as he pulled her down the sidewalk toward his Jag. They were no help, especially David, who was grinning broadly rather than coming to her rescue—the big traitor.

"I like him, Liv," he called with a wave as Joseph tucked her in the passenger seat and shut the door.

"I love him," she whispered in the empty car as her determined dominant rounded the hood. "Although I have a feeling my bottom won't by the end of the night."

THE CRACK OF HIS BROAD palm on one upturned cheek echoed through the bedroom. The sound hadn't died when his hand connected on the other side with another crack. And that's how it went as he kept up a steady barrage of crisp, stingy swats, too numerous to count, that brought tears to her eyes and stole her breath. When he finally stopped, he rubbed his hand from the crest of her cheeks to the top of her thighs, dispersing the heat and easing some of the sting.

"What have you learned, pet?"

"That honesty is the best policy, sir."

His hand tightened on her ass. "Are you being flippant? Not a wise idea with my hand still on your ass."

"I wasn't being flippant," she rushed to explain, even though she was, sort of. "I've learned that being honest is so much easier than trying to keep up with lies and concealing secrets. It's less stressful than worrying when the truth will come out because it always does, especially for me."

He ran his nails lightly over sensitive skin, making her shiver. The near perpetual desire Joseph inspired, with a softly spoken command in his smooth baritone, a heated glance, or a touch, whether for pleasure or discipline, flooded her pussy with liquid heat. She was more than ready for him to disburse the fire he'd instilled with his hand to the rest of her body by driving into her and taking her fast and hard.

"Is that all?"

"No. It's a whole lot less embarrassing to be honest, even though it's hard sometimes, than having your friends spill the beans."

"I had hoped you would have learned a deeper meaning, one that was less egocentric."

She frowned. That meant selfish, didn't it?

Before she could replay her answer and determine what had made him think that, he gripped her hips and helped her up from his lap.

"Kneel on the bench, hands flat on the bed, ass nice and high. I'll be right back."

She looked at the padded bench at the foot of the bed, where he pulled her over his thighs and spanked her thoroughly. Kneeling on it would put her at a good height for him to take her from behind like she wanted, but she had a feeling that wasn't what he had in mind. She turned to see him emerge from the big walk-in closet, a long cardboard box in hand. Her brows knitted together in confusion. When had he brought that home and why, after already being punished was he bringing it out now?

"In position, pet," he ordered as he dropped the box on the bed and withdrew the riding crop.

"But...you just punished me, master."

"I did, but those swats were for David. You heard me promise him a few licks, didn't you?"

Her hands flew back to her fiery backside. Which, of course, he saw. He moved toward her, and once in front of her, removed her hands from her bottom and placed them on his chest.

"Any rubbing that's done tonight is up to me. Understood?"

"Yes, master," she whispered.

He tucked the crop under his arm and framed her face with his hands. "Are you beginning to see how much trouble you're in, pet?"

She nodded and squeaked, "I think so."

"Let's be clear. This punishment isn't because of choices you made in your past, and it has nothing to do with the bastard poser you were involved with or what you had to do to get over his abuse. This is solely for lying by omission and keeping secrets from me and your friend, who has been your protector for years. Dishonesty isn't something I will tolerate, Olivia, and your backside will endure the brunt of my displeasure until you figure that out."

"But I do, sir. That's to say, I have. Figured it out, I mean."

"Mmm," he replied, sounding skeptical. Then he removed all doubt by stating, "I'm not so sure."

He kissed her forehead gently then released her and tapped the bench smartly with the crop.

"In position, naughty girl. Your punishment from me is just beginning."

On her hands and knees, quivering ass pointed high as she awaited further castigation, she had a moment for introspection. Maybe she had been too single-minded when considering what keeping her past from Joseph meant, or the risks she taken going to clubs on her own where she knew no one. In this case, because she found the dom she'd always wanted, the end justified the means, but neither of the doms in her life, nor Emma, found the means and the risks she taken acceptable.

The leather square on the end of the crop, tapping gently, signaled the start of round two.

"I think a dozen might help clear your head, and perhaps you'll find a better answer to my question."

"I'm nervous, sir. I'm not so sure."

The taps over both cheeks and her upper thighs grew crisper, although they lacked the bite that she knew from experience a crop could deliver.

"You're an intelligent woman, Olivia," her master drawled. "If you focus hard, I'm certain it will come to you."

But it didn't. Not after receiving twelve stinging strokes—he used the leather keeper instead of the rod, applying it sharply, and with deliberation, never striking the same spot twice—on her cheeks and thighs.

Again, when he stopped, his hands moved over her skin, lightly rubbing and stroking in a soothing après-spank massage.

"What have you learned, pet?" he asked, repeating the same question as before.

"That you wield a mean crop master and your aftercare is phenomenal."

His open hand rained down on her twice-punished butt. Olivia hissed and shrieked her apologies, sincerely regretting that this time she had been flippant, while he delivered three searing spanks on each side.

She was panting for breath and doing her best to stay still, when his hands resumed the sensual, and beyond sublime, massage.

"Now, then. How about a serious answer this time?"

What had she learned about honesty that wasn't solely centered on her?

"Trust!" she blurted out. "By being honest with you and David and Emma, I prove I'm trustworthy. I failed at that miserably the night I went to Decadence. When my escort canceled and I went on alone, I knew that was something David would never condone and that he would be furious when he found out."

"When?" he challenged.

"No," she whispered. "If, because I didn't plan on telling him."

"Very good, pet. That was an honest answer. You were correct before when you said the truth always comes out. Can you think of any other reasons honesty is best?"

She hesitated, trying to focus her brain away from his hands on her ass, and how his thumbs kept grazing her pussy. The touch, inadvertent or deliberate, was fleeting, enough to arouse but not get her off. Darn dastardly dom.

He patted her gently then his hands fell away. "You think on that during round three."

Tall and handsome and well in command of her and her punishment, Joseph came into view when he walked around the corner of the bed. His destination was the box, and she watched in dread as he pulled out the cane.

His eyes met hers. "Six should help you come up with another answer."

Then he strode out of sight, the distinctive whish of the cane as he tested it making her shiver. She'd already had a taste of what Astrid and the other subs at the club feared from Master J. When he used it before he was furious. Tonight, he seemed more disappointed than angry.

The soft whisper as the cane cut through the air was the only warning she got before a line of fire blazed across both cheeks.

Holy crap! her mind screamed while the only audible sound she made, a hiss as she sucked air into her lungs replacing what had whooshed out with the cane stroke. How quickly she'd forgotten its bite and sting.

Another followed about an inch below the first. He let her absorb the sensation for a solid minute then delivered cane stroke number three below the other two.

Pausing, he ran his hands over the parallel lines of fire. "Halfway there," he murmured. "Gotta say, baby. You take punishment like you were born for it, even the cane."

"Thank you, sir?" she squeaked.

She thought she heard him chuckle, but his voice was even when he asked, "Red, yellow, or green, pet. Give me a color before we proceed."

"Much as I hate to admit it, I'm green, sir."

"Ah...there's the honesty we've been getting at. By telling me the truth, it helps me gauge how to proceed. Trust is a two-way street between dom and sub, whether during punishment or play." His divine hands fell away. "Ready for the last three?"

"No...sir."

"Hm, then you couldn't be green."

"But I am, sir," was her immediately replied. "I'm green because this is punishment for disappointing you and David and Emma. I'm able and willing to accept it, but that doesn't mean I'm ready, or that I have to like it, does it?"

His low chuckle was audible this time. "No, it doesn't, pet. And, I have to say, that was an even better answer than the last. But let's get this done."

The swish of the cane sounded three times as, in quick succession, he delivered the last three strokes. Livia yelped and hissed and promised to the be the epitome of honesty and trustworthiness as lines of searing flames moved down her ass, the last traversing both sit spots.

He lifted her in his arms and carried her not to the bench but to the super comfortable overstuffed chair in the corner. This signaled that the punishment session was well and truly over. While he held her, wrapped in a furry throw, and urged her to drink the water he'd set out in advance, his hand on her ass used the fur to soothe and comfort.

Her eyes had drifted shut when he rose and moved from the chair to the bed. He stretched her out on her stomach, sat beside her hip, and applied a cooling cream to her cheeks. Aftercare was wonderful, but it always seemed ironic to her that these doms, like Joseph, who could be so strict with discipline were often bigger sticklers about the TLC that followed.

"I swear, master. No more secrets or omissions, and I promise, there are no more skeletons in my past to expose. Can you forgive me?"

He leaned forward and pressed his lips against the small of her back. "I already have, little one. You screwed up, but you paid the price earlier tonight when confronted with your lies and omissions, and just now with my hand, crop, and cane. Now we start fresh with a clean slate."

"That makes me happy."

"Me, too," he whispered, dotting more kisses along her spine. "I won't ask again what you learned because, by your answer, you learned plenty, but one specific answer I was looking for tonight was respect, pet."

"Yes, of course." She rolled onto her side and gazed up at him. "I respect you, Joseph, at home, at work, at play. I'm sorry if through my actions I implied I didn't."

"Apology accepted, pet. But think about this and take it to heart. Honesty, whether in an intimate relationship or friendship, builds a foundation of trust, and shows respect for another. If you respect and love someone, you want to be honest, so what you have endures."

Tears filled her eyes. "I want to build that foundation strong, master, by always being honest and showing you my love and respect, so we endure. You should give me six more," she declared, inching toward the edge of the bed. "I deserve it for not realizing that on my own."

He stopped her, easing her onto her stomach again. "Who is the master here, pet?"

"You are, sir."

"Correct. The master determines the punishment and when enough is enough. You're done, baby." He resumed the massage and gentle kisses. "Except for me taking care of you."

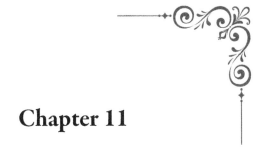

Chapter 11

ON MONDAY, WHEN SHE and Joseph drove downtown and walked into the office together, things had changed for Livia. She no longer cared who suspected something was going on between them, or what rumors were flying, or if anyone saw the soft looks they shared or when he ran a finger down her cheek in the softest of caresses, which made her heart melt.

They weren't over the top with PDA. Like he once said, he had no intention of doing it on her desk with the door open. They were still professional, but no longer willing to hide their love for one another.

By the end of the day, the office was still standing, and the HR director's head hadn't exploded. Being proactive, Joseph had called her and warned her, as well as the other partners, which helped. She had to admit it was more pleasant and much less stressful than the previous weeks when she'd felt distanced from him and little more than a dirty secret. She'd also gotten a helluva lot more work done.

"Ready to go?"

She glanced up and smiled, watching Joseph, briefcase in hand, shrugging into his suit coat.

"I just shut down," she replied as she stood. "Just gotta get my purse."

When she bent to retrieve it from the bottom drawer, she felt his gaze. Peering at him over her shoulder, she found him staring at the back of her skirt.

He grinned, unashamed. "Not that I don't enjoy it, baby. But you don't have to wave your gorgeous round ass in my face anymore. I'm a sure thing."

Her laughter bubbled up as she straightened and slid her arm through the shoulder strap of her Michael Kors knockoff red leather tote.

"I was going to store it somewhere more convenient. But after three years, this is the only place it fits."

She strolled up to him and standing close, laid her hand against his five-o'clock beard-shadowed face. "I hope continuing to wave my behind in your face won't be too much of a hardship, Mr. Hooks."

He bent and claimed her lips in a whisper-soft kiss full of promise. "I think I can cope, Ms. Wright. Dinner at Moonshine's?" he asked as he wrapped an arm around her waist and escorted her out. "Or would you prefer ordering in?"

"Moonshine's," she declared decisively. "Now that we're out there for the world to see, no more skulking around. Besides, since you mentioned it, I have a taste for their Creole shrimp and grits."

They walked through the lobby, drawing several interested looks. Joseph apparently couldn't care less, his hand dipping lower to ride the upper curves of her bottom as he opened the door and let her precede him. She grinned up at him as she passed, laughing when he winked down at her, because with him by her side, unashamedly professing his desire and love for her often, she didn't give a hoot, either.

ON WEDNESDAY, THEY left thirty minutes early from work. After a quick stop at his place to change out of boring office wear, they were in his Jag, making the eighty-mile trip south on I-35 to San Antonio. This time, Joseph promised she'd tour the Decadence dungeon before he carried her off to a private room and had his wicked way with her.

With him as company, the drive was much more pleasant and passed in no time. Another bonus: she didn't have to wait in the long check-in line for guests. On a club member's arm, she was in the crowded lobby within minutes. But as she passed the club and fetwear-bedecked submissives eager to make it into the inner sanctum, whether out of curiosity or hoping to find the dom or domme of their dreams, she imagined she'd had the same mix of excitement and anxiety on her face a few short weeks ago.

Astrid was behind the counter once again, her eyes going from her to Joseph in wonder. Remembering how the sub had reacted at being assigned to Master J for punishment, she gave the girl a sad shake of her head. She didn't know what she was missing, and Livia was grateful for that.

Had things gone differently that night, if fate hadn't intervened, if her mentor hadn't become ill, or if Astrid had accepted Joseph as her disciplinarian for the night, her life as she knew it could have been drastically different.

"Ready, pet?" he asked, his voice warm with affection.

She loved when he called her that.

Glancing up, she met his twinkling green gaze without the barrier of his glasses. He had contacts in which, who knew, he'd had for years. He made an imposing figure in his black suit, not tweed tonight, and he'd foregone the tie, bow, or otherwise. The monochromatic effect added height to his already tall frame.

He caught her hand and pulled her close in the crush of people. "You're quiet, Livia," he observed. "Is everything all right?"

"Yes, but it's a little overwhelming. Being here with you, it's like the first time and seems more real, somehow."

"It is real. But you're safe with me," he assured her, lifting her hand to his lips. Expecting the soft brush of his mouth on the back like usual, he flipped it at the last second, giving her palm and the inside of her wrist a warm kiss. Shivers of desire coursed through her when she felt the tip of his tongue on her skin.

"This is supposed to be fun, pet," he reminded her.

Joseph didn't lead her directly to the playroom. Instead, he opened the door to the lounge. A wave of music blasted her in the face. She looked toward the stage and saw the girls up front once again.

"I thought you'd like to say hello to your friends, have a drink, and relax a bit after the drive before we go into the playroom?"

"Can we?" She grinned up at him. He was always so considerate of her needs. Any other man she'd been with would have dragged her directly to the dungeon like a caveman, beating his chest and demanding his gratification. Not Joseph.

"Don't sound so relieved."

"I didn't mean it like that. I'm excited to see the playroom, but—"

"I was teasing, baby. Come on."

It took several minutes to wend their way through the crowd and by the time they did, Elena and her band were taking their first break. As before, the sound level decreased dramatically as the lights came up.

Mara spotted them first as they approached.

"You came back," she exclaimed, a smile lighting her face. It turned quickly to surprise as she took in the man behind her. Her gaze shifted quickly back to Livia and homed in on the leather and lace encircling her neck.

Her fingers, as if with a mind of their own, rose to the leather band at her throat. Her new collar was unlike any she'd ever seen. Not in the traditional style but Victorian-inspired. He'd presented it to her earlier while she stood in front of the mirror getting dressed.

In need of help with her zipper, she'd lifted her hair. Instead of going to her lower back to do her up, his fingers brushed her nape. When she glanced up, he was wrapping a leather collar, trimmed in lace with heart-shaped nickel accents around her neck.

While he'd adjusted the fit, she smiled through a mist of tears, overjoyed to wear the outward sign of his possession.

"This collar is for play. I know we're still new, but I want to see you in a permanent collar soon; one that you can wear everywhere, every day."

"I'd love that, master." As her fingers traced the intricately tooled leather and the delicate lace, her eyes met his in the glass. When she could speak, her voice was husky with emotion. "This is beautiful. Where did you find it?"

"A BDSM friendly leather artist the club uses made it special for me. She does exquisite work." He turned her, lifting her face for his kiss. *"There is something else that goes with it."*

He held up a heart-shaped lock in antique gold in one hand and a key in the other. The lock he attached it to, a tiny ring in the buckle of her collar, closing it with a little snick.

"This stays in place, pet. Until your master removes it." He pocketed the gold skeleton key. *"There are matching cuffs. Give me your wrists."*

As he buckled them in place, he pressed a kiss in each palm.

"So, Master J—" Mara's voice snapped her back to the present, as did Joseph's hand tightening on her hip. Her new friend's gaze switched between her and the man at her back, grinning broadly. "You've claimed our Livia already?"

"I have, little felon. Has Sean been keeping you out of trouble?"

"I'm trying, Joe, but it's a full-time job." A familiar male voice shifted her attention to the tall dom who had rescued her from the lobby the first night. He came up behind his submissive wife and surrounded her in a full body hug. His eyes fell to Livia, taking in her collar and Joseph's arm around her waist. "You work fast, my friend. I'm impressed. I think it might be a club record."

"Don't alert Guinness Book just yet. I had an inside edge."

Joseph's remark came with a chuckle. The melodic sound reverberated from his chest, to where he pressed against her back, and then radiated pleasantly throughout her body. She leaned against him, enjoying their closeness.

"Master Joseph's edge is that he's her boss," Mara explained.

"Is he now?" Sean replied, an intrigued glint in his blue eyes. "Sounds like there's a story here. Fill me in over a scotch? I think we still have some of that swill you and Cap enjoy so much."

Livia saw him nod readily but paused just as quick, eyeing the pitchers of what had to be margaritas on the table. "One normal-sized drink this time, pet," he ordered. "I want you clearheaded. After the show, we'll tour the dungeon and find somewhere to play."

She smiled up at him, dutifully answering, "Yes, master."

The next thing she knew, he had her bent over his arm in a clinch worthy of an old Hollywood heartthrob.

Left dizzy and aroused, he assisted her to a chair as the girls made room for her at their table. Then he was off to the bar with Sean, both men quickly swallowed up by the crowd.

"Don't you love/hate when they do that?" Elena laughed as she joined them.

Lexie, who was nearest the pitcher, poured each of the new arrivals a drink. "You look like you could use one of these—stat." With a welcoming smile, she slid a filled-to-the-rim glass in front of her. "So, you and Master J... Dish, girl."

She was about to spill her guts when Megan joined them. Her strikingly handsome dominant husband seated her, sank his hand in her hair, used it to tug her head back, and kissed her like he would swallow her whole. Then, with a nod to the group, he took off toward the bar like the other men.

"Is drop-dead gorgeous a requirement for the masters in this place?" Livia asked as she stared after him.

"I think we've all asked that same question. Just wait until you get in the dungeon where they're half dressed," Megan warned, fanning herself with her hand.

"I'm a little nervous about that," Livia admitted. "I didn't make it to the dungeon the last time I was here."

"No kidding," Mara replied. "You hightailed it out of here like your thong was on fire. As soon as you busted through the front doors, I saw Joseph in hot pursuit. I would have paid money to be a fly on the wall in the lobby that night."

"Ooo, do tell," Megan gushed with a grin. "Did he chase you down and toss you over his shoulder? I freakin' love when Tony does that."

"I don't know if I'd call it a chase, exactly. He caught up with me at the door. I fainted and later woke up in his bed. About the over-the-shoulder part, I'd have to ask."

"These Decadence masters," Mara said with a dreamy look on her face, clearly lost in a romantic memory of her own. "Where else in the world could you find so many gorgeous men all with the power to sweep a girl off her feet?"

"Yeah," Megan sighed. "They also spank you, tie you to the bed, fuck you senseless, and convince you that you can't live without them. We don't stand a chance."

Feminine heads nodded in agreement all around and Livia, who thought it only happened to her, laughed with relief.

"SORRY, PET. BUT YOU part ways with your shoes here."

Any other time, she would have protested leaving her prized Valentino sling-back pointy-toe pumps anywhere. She'd found them gently used at a consignment shop for a fourth of their original thousand-dollar price tag, but $250 on a legal secretary's budget was a lot. But she held onto Joseph's arm to take them off and handed them over, too busy trying to take in everything about the ginormous dungeon behind him.

Affectionately referred to as the playroom by the members, it was huge, lavish, and when she got a good look at the first few stations, completely depraved. It made the other BDSM clubs she'd been to, which were all public access, dim in comparison. As she walked the circuit with her dom—what the members called the walkway that wound between the roped-off stations filling the vast playroom—Livia didn't know where to look first. Did she watch the exhibitionists under the spotlights on the elevated stages, clearly reveling in their love of being watched? Or the inverted male sub hanging by a cable from the ceiling? He was strapped to a spreader bar by the ankles, revolving slowly as his mistress methodically flogged his naked body everywhere.

There was a scene at a bondage table where the dom was making his bound submissive scream in ecstasy as he dripped hot wax on her breasts and between her splayed legs. In another station, they had dimmed the overhead spotlight to better see the purplish wand that buzzed and crackled as a dom moved it over his subs bound and trembling body.

When Joseph paused to watch a trio at a chain station, he positioned her in front of him so she, too, could see. With his arms wrapped around her, and their bodies pressed together, she couldn't miss the hard length of him nudging her lower back. She knew he liked restraints, and impact play, and control, but wondered about his other kinks. Did he like group play, like the ménage taking place in front of them?

The sub was beautiful, with alabaster skin and full curves. She was bare except for a black waist cincher that laced up the back. Her wrist cuffs were hooked to a chain, stretching her hands high above her head and forcing her up on her toes. With her eyes closed, lips parted, chest rising and falling rapidly, her moans rose over the din of the room likely because of the man with his face buried between her spread thighs. Interspersed with her moans was an uninhibited throaty cry every time the third, another man, lashed her back, ass, and thighs.

"What is he using, master?"

"That is an Alley Cat, a variation of a cat 'o nine tails. The braided and knotted ends up the intensity from a standard flogger. It's light and fast and packs quite a bite. Monroe is skilled with it. Notice her skin. It's pink, but without a single welt."

"She seems to enjoy it."

An understatement, Livia thought, as another joyful cry rose from the submissive. As she looked on in fascination, the dom dropped his lash and tore open his leathers. After spitting on his fingers and wetting the head of his cock, he thrust into her from behind. As if planned, the other dom rose and with her legs draped over his forearms, he entered her from the front. Simultaneously, the two men pumped away while a sustained wail rose from the submissive wedged between them.

It didn't end there, however. The man in the rear, literally, fisted her hair and twisted her head for his kiss while the man in front plumped up a breast and latched onto her nipple. It was raw, visceral, and more erotic than anything Livia had ever witnessed. The public clubs she'd visited didn't allow full nudity or sex. Club Decadence, being private was on a whole other level.

Livia took a step back but didn't get far with her dom directly behind her.

Kudos to the woman. Even though the scene was provocative and beyond exciting, it was more than she could ever imagine taking on herself, nor would she want to. Joseph alone stretched her limits. She couldn't see herself handling two men at a time.

Joseph's hand cupped her chin and angled her face up to his. The spotlights over the stations cast the circuit in shadow. Even in the dimness, his green eyes flashed when he stated, "The scene is intense, sensual, carnal, hot, and a bunch of other adjectives, pet, but I don't share—ever."

She twisted in his arms and buried her face in his chest. "You don't know how relieved that makes me, sir. I couldn't..."

"Just another way we suit." As the trio's cries of release filled the air, Joseph led her away. "Let's move on. There's more to see."

Next stop was a spanking bench with one dom and one sub. She was facedown and restrained at her wrists and knees while he took her vigorously from behind.

"BDSM 101, essentially," she uttered, relieved to find something more her speed.

The dom paused briefly and picked up a mini-flogger from on a nearby table. In profile, she recognized Master Dex. Her eyes dropped instantly to the sub...Elena.

She sighed in relief, which made him chuckle. "You prefer monogamy and fidelity, it seems. It also says something that you see a spanking bench and a mini-flogger as run of the mill."

"Decadence is much more intense than anywhere I've ever been. It's refreshing to see something old school."

"Be glad we didn't find them in Dex's corner." He nodded to a large cordoned-off area up ahead. "He's a whip master, the single tail being his tool of choice."

Looking from the wooden whipping post in the shadowed corner to the petite singer restrained over the bench, Livia shook her head in amazement. "But she's so small, and he's...huge and strong. How does she handle that?"

"Different strokes, as they say." Sounding amused by his pun, he once again moved them deeper inside the cavernous playroom. "I reserved us a room upstairs."

Her attention turned to the stairs ahead of them leading to the open second floor.

Reading her unconcealed curiosity, he explained, "The second floor houses a dozen private rooms, each with a different theme. Some are so popular they have to be reserved weeks in advance. I was hoping for the Sultan's Chamber, but it is the most sought-after room, so we'll have to make do with what was available. Sean and Dex told me they're expanding because what they have is simply not enough to keep up with the demand. A dozen more will be open in the next six months. We'll be able to play sultan and concubine, one night, headmaster and unruly student the next, or perhaps, doctor."

"Doctor!" she repeated, eyes wide, her mind reeling with kinky possibilities.

"You're intrigued," he deduced correctly. "I'll have to sign us up for the exam room next."

They had arrived at the bottom of the stairs where a dungeon monitor was limiting access. Joseph took her hand before proceeding. "I thought you'd prefer a private room to the main floor on your first trip."

She nodded. "Thank you, master. This is all quite unexpected and rather intimidating."

"We'll go slowly for now, little one. Once you become more comfortable, I'd like to see you on the cross." He tipped his head, indicating the St. Andrew's Cross behind him and the intense flogging scene going on. Staring glassy-eyed at the leather tails that rose and fell across the restrained submissive's breasts, she swallowed hard.

He pressed a kiss to the corner of her parted lips. "When you're ready," he reassured her. "Tonight, it's only me and you, and a room full of surprises."

THE WALL SCONCES WERE aglow, the special bulbs flickering and casting a candlelit ambiance over the chamber. As Joseph stepped inside, he turned to watch Livia's reaction to the Tudor Throne Room.

As he'd hoped, her animated face conveyed her delight. Her eyes shone with excitement and a becoming blush of pink had risen in her cheeks. The quickening of her breathing drew his eyes to the front of her dress where her taut nipples were visible through the clingy fabric. Her arousal spurred his own, but he couldn't get much harder than he already was and had been all evening.

"Through the door is a dressing room where you'll find costumes. Choose something that suits the room and your mood."

Joseph grinned as she sprang forward, practically racing across the room. Role-play obviously appealed to his submissive. As the door closed behind her, he turned and surveyed the opulent room, which he'd seen before but only briefly.

The centerpiece was the huge four-poster bed. Calling them posts was misleading; they were more like columns with Tudor-style carvings, and he doubted it was typical of the era to have eyebolts bolted into the wood for restraints. Although he could be wrong.

Moving toward it for a closer look, he suspected the two columns at the foot of the bed could double as whipping posts. The room had sufficient space to enact a whipping scene, but that wasn't his taste. The bed had other features he was eager to test out with his lovely pet's assistance.

The bed was immense, larger than a standard king-size frame. He imagined it could hold most of the royal court if the king had the inclination. Again, not his thing, but he and Livia would put the wide surface to good use. She'd adore the gold and red linens and the stack of cushy pillows, which would be ideal for propping and draping and lifting certain curvy body parts up.

On the opposite side of the room, a red velvet throne sat on a raised dais. It was the perfect place for his majesty to inspect his subject or be entertained by a dance. There was a padded stool tucked beneath the ornate chair, the sight of which conjured an image of Livia kneeling naked on the plush velvet, her hands bound behind her back as she paid homage to her sovereign lord with her inventive mouth and tongue.

Joseph smiled, looking forward to bringing his fantasy to life, as he crossed to the storage armoire to get his accessories for the night. Inside, he found everything he could possibly need to make Livia scream with pleasure or, if he chose—beg for mercy. On hooks, inside the double doors, was a variety of short-tail whips and canes. He passed on both. The former was too harsh for her delicate, flawless skin; the latter too much like punishment. He had only pleasure planned for her tonight.

He selected one of the many branding paddles—the Tudors had a penchant for marking criminals back in the day—a single word in raised lettering adorning each wooden blade. Joseph passed over *slut* and *mine*, grinning when he came to one with *pet* embossed in bold script. Perfect.

He tucked it under his arm, while slipping a few other odds and ends into his pockets. As he was finishing, the door opened behind him.

Livia stood in the doorway, illuminated by the light behind her. She likely didn't know that her long burgundy gown—off-the-shoulder with puffy sleeves, a fitted bodice, and a full flowing skirt common to the era—was sheer and revealed her shapely legs, from her ankles to the apex of her thighs. Atop her gleaming blonde hair, which was long and loose as he liked it, she wore a circlet of gold. He gazed at her appreciatively, his eyes scanning every exquisite inch.

His inspection must have been overlong because she began to fidget. "You're gorgeous, pet," he reassured.

Smoothing down the fabric, she smiled. "It was this or a servant's costume. I preferred being the queen tonight."

"And so you shall be." Her blush lit the room more effectively than the wall sconces. "If Her Royal Highness will stand in the middle of the room and wait for me, I'll finish preparations."

It took only a moment for him to place his tools where he needed them, on the nightstand and in a pouch that conveniently hung off the side of the throne. Last, he slipped off his shirt and into a long, flowing velvet robe, which he left open in front. It was regal but ridiculous. Still, when in Rome...

Joining her in the middle of the room, he stood close but not touching. If she inhaled deeply, her erect nipples would graze his bare chest.

Her eyes dropped to his shoulders then swept down his front. "I like the robe; it's stately. You're only lacking a crown, Your Majesty."

With gentle fingers, he skimmed over her bare shoulders and across her collarbone to her throat where he traced the leather and lace. "Your cuffs and collar are from a different time, but they go nicely, I think."

He dipped his head, pressed kisses along his fingers' path. With practiced movements, he raised her hands and hooked her wrists to the velvet-encased chains above her head. With her head tilted back, she watched as he expanded the telescoping spreader bar between the two restraints, leaving her upper body open and vulnerable to him.

"You are well and truly caught, my queen." Slowly, he trailed his hands down her arms, his fingers following the edge of her gown to the low bodice and with a quick tug, pulled the stretchy material below her breasts. His avid gaze took in the abundance now bare and presented prettily before him. Unable to wait, he palmed their fullness with both hands, his thumbs sweeping sensually across the perfect pink tips.

"Joseph." His name was little more than a sexy exhale.

He tweaked a nipple at her lapse. "You will address your king respectfully or face the court's displeasure. I think sire is appropriate while in my throne room."

"Yes, Sire," she breathed, a small grin tilting her lips as she leaned into him for more.

"Queen Olivia likes nipple play. Let me give them the royal treatment."

With a hand at her back to keep her still, he dipped his head and took one hard nipple into his mouth. Opening wide, he applied suction, while inside, he lashed the tip with his tongue. His free hand cupped her other breast, pinching and rolling the nipple, tugging gently at intervals.

Her moans conveyed her enjoyment, as did the muffled clanking of the velvet-encased chains high overhead. She trembled beneath his touch, the shuddering rush of air through her lips becoming harsh as her need grew. When he stopped momentarily and moved to the other nipple, to lavish it with the equal attention, her whimpers became more insistent.

"Now," he murmured, when he raised his head minutes later, "for the presentation of the crown jewels."

He held up nipple clamps with sapphire-like stones dangling from delicate chains.

Despite her obvious arousal, she giggled.

"Do you find something amusing, my queen?"

"Other *jewels* came to mind."

"Naughty wench," he scolded, tweaking a nipple.

This time, she laughed outright. "Please, Sire. Don't make me laugh. I'd hate for you to be insulted. I can't imagine the punishment for such a crime."

"For an unguarded tongue, ten lashes at the whipping post was the order of the day."

This sobered her and she protested on an indrawn breath, "A whip. But, Joseph—"

"But for my queen, nothing so harsh. An hour in the brank should suffice, I think."

"The what?"

"Look on the shelves behind me."

He watched as she scanned the back wall.

"Also known as the Gossip's Bridle."

He knew the instant she located the padded head cage with the penis gag. Horror-stricken, she slipped her role. "You can't be serious. I wouldn't be able to breathe."

"Are you ready to safeword?"

Her eyes met his with obvious dismay. "Is that my only choice?"

"If I say it is."

She snapped her mouth shut, closing her eyes as well.

"Stoic is my queen," he murmured. "Back in Henry Tudor's day, the cage was metal, and the gag had barbs. A damn unpleasant piece of business."

"Forgive me, but how do you know so much about fifteenth-century torture?"

"Sixteenth. I was a history major in undergrad and took several classes on the Renaissance. Henry was a cruel bastard and had nothing on De Sade, but never would I be so harsh with you." He applied the first clamp as he said this, adjusting the tightness until she squirmed and tried to pull away. "Would you rather have the Bridle?"

When she shook her head, he backed off the pressure just a bit.

"You're holding your breath, pet. Breathe through the initial pain and it will even out."

Carefully, he observed as she did as he bade. After a moment, she relaxed.

"Better?"

"Yes, Sire. It's been a long time since I've worn clamps. I'd forgotten."

He flicked the dangling blue gems while pinching her other nipple. Knowing what to expect this time, Livia managed the application of the other clamp with ease and grace.

He turned her until she faced the mirrored back wall. "These enhance your beautiful breasts to perfection and match the blue of your eyes." As he caressed her from behind, he licked up the side of her neck and latched onto her earlobe. Huskily, he advised, "I quite like them, so prepare to be clamped often."

Her head fell back on his shoulder while he kissed and played. Soon, his need for her was a throbbing ache pressing hard against his zipper. He released her wrists from the chains above and linked them behind her back. He further restricted her movement by tugging her bodice down to her waist and her sleeves to her elbows, which trapped her arms next to her body.

Leading her to the throne, he pulled out the padded stool. He then settled into his elaborate chair and took a moment to absorb her beauty.

When she became restless under his scrutiny, he smiled and issued his first of many kingly edicts. "I require entertainment, my queen. Kneel for me."

She attempted to, struggling with her descent because of her long gown, which essentially hobbled her. His hands shot out, grasping her hips to steady her before she fell flat on her face. Once he'd settled her on the tufted bench, he admired the pretty picture she made—cheeks flushed, clamped nipples now a beautiful berry red, breasts quivering delectably with the rapid rise and fall of her chest. When her tongue slipped out, gliding across her lower lip and wetting it, his smile faded. It was all he could do not to quit the game, throw her to the floor, and fuck her.

"Release my cock, my beautiful queen," he growled hungrily, "using only your luscious mouth."

He watched in fascination as she leaned forward and nudged aside the halves of his robe with her chin. Underneath, he wore only trousers. Her head moved to his waistband, but rather than diving right into the button, she opened her mouth and licked his navel. Although not what he'd asked, he allowed her to play, curious to see what his little imp would do next.

His abdomen tightened and his chest filled with a sharply indrawn breath as she moved higher, following the thin line of dark hair from his abdomen to his chest, where she shifted to tongue a nipple.

"You have the body of an Olympian. Long..." She paused to lick. "Lean..." she breathed, catching the small bud between her teeth. "And whipcord strong."

She applied suction, swirling her tongue first left then right.

"I love how you're all sinew and lean muscle," she exclaimed softly, her husky voice making his cock jerk. She moved across his chest to the other side. "Do you swim?"

"I do," he answered with a low groan, "three times a week."

"It certainly shows. My king... So. Very. Sexy." She punctuated each word with torturous swirls of her tongue, taxing his composure.

His hands shot to his trousers, which he unbuttoned and unzipped in a flash. "Stop teasing and suck me."

Her head came up, and she grinned. "It would be my royal pleasure, Your Majesty."

Her mouth engulfed him, taking most of his length in one glide. As she pulled off, she angled her head and licked down his length, using the flat of her tongue along the underside. She slid back up, encircling the head round and round. Next, she began sucking, taking him to the back of her throat before withdrawing, nearly coming off all the way, teasing as if she would, but never losing him.

Flipping off the gold circlet, he wove his fingers through the silken strands of her hair. Gathering it in a fist at the back of her head gave him an unobstructed view of his cock gliding in and out of her full, pink lips, her hot, wet mouth applying the perfect amount of suction.

Too soon, the familiar tingling stirred in his balls, signaling he was close. He fought for control, not willing to give in so quickly. He wasn't a kid anymore, but his sex drive was strong. Livia stirred him like no other woman ever had. If he blew now, he'd be ready for round two within the hour.

His fingers tightened around her head as he pumped his hips to meet her bobbing mouth. He came in a surge of heat, his hips arching off the chair, sending him deeper as he shuddered and shouted his release. Collapsing the next moment, he closed his eyes, savoring the warm, gentle licks of her tongue.

When he had recovered somewhat, he reached for her, hands capturing her beneath the arms and hauling her onto his lap, cuddling her close. "My queen has beauty and a wickedly talented mouth. I am a lucky monarch."

"Thank you, Sire, for the compliment and for allowing me to polish your royal scepter." She buried her face in his neck and giggled. Her good mood was infectious and made him chuckle, but he couldn't allow such sass from a lowly subject and added a teasing swat to her covered backside.

"Oh, Your Highness, when you spank me thusly, you give me a royal flush." That sent her into peals of laughter.

"You, my pet, are becoming a royal pain in the arse."

She hooted, mirth-filled tears rolling down her cheeks. "Oh, Your Majesty, that was a jolly good one."

He shook his head, although he was grinning broadly. Clasping her firmly in his arms, he rose to his feet and strode across the room to the bed. He dropped her carefully, so she landed facedown and not on her still bound hands. She landed with a muffled "*oomph.*"

The grunt quickly turned into more giggles as she rolled to her side. Breathless, she flipped her hair out of her face, which was glowing, alive with both color and laughter.

With a knee in the mattress, he rolled her closer.

"Let's lose the gown." Joseph unhooked her wrist restraints and, in a blink, had the gown undone and off. "Scoot up on the pillows."

While she did as she was told, he shrugged off his robe, toed off his shoes, and shucked his trousers. Then he followed, stalking her on hands and knees.

"I don't know if you noticed, but the king's bed has a special head and footboard."

She craned her neck back to see. Her brows gathered as she pondered the padded headboard. "I'm probably crazy for asking, but what are the holes for?"

"Let me show you." He crawled up farther and knelt by her head. "Arms up."

Immediately, she raised them. Joseph lifted the upper portion of the panel and captured her wrists in the center two circles. Once he slid it back into place, they weren't going anywhere.

"It's a pillory. Also, common to the Tudor era. Usually it's set out in the town square, but for our purposes, someone cleverly incorporated it into the bed." He lay down beside her and began stroking her body slowly all over. "Much more comfortable, don't you think?"

"I thought that was a stock."

"No, a pillory usually involves the feet as well."

He smiled when she lifted her head and eyed the footboard at least a foot shy of her own two feet.

"It appears they designed it for a taller sub than me or with a man in mind." She glanced up at him. "Perhaps the king?"

He barked with laughter. "The day I'm hand and foot in a pillory is the day I abdicate my throne. The middle section is adjustable, so it can accommodate pipsqueak subs like you." He rolled off the bed. "I have another method that's less involved, however."

He crossed to the armoire, opening and closing drawers until he found what he wanted. Back with her quickly, he applied ankle cuffs. With the fingers of one hand tucked in the leather restraints, he lifted her legs, bending her almost double as he found the velvet loops at the upper posts. With the help of a quick release clasp, he easily had her legs spread and linked to the top corners.

He sat back and admired his handiwork. "Comfy, my queen?"

She snorted, wordlessly telling him what she thought of his questions. "Do you plan to do this often? If so, I'll need to resume my yoga classes. I'm not as limber as I used to be."

Serious now, he leaned over her, meeting her gaze steadily. "Is that a yes or a no, Livia? I don't want you strained or in pain."

Chapter 12

AS SHE LAY THERE, FOLDED in half like a taco shell, her ass and all her girly parts open for business, Livia realized she and Joseph had very different definitions of comfortable. Still, she saw his concern and promptly answered, "Comfy enough, master."

"Good. I don't want undue pressure on any joints or cramped muscles. On the other hand, I wouldn't want you to be too comfortable. What would be the fun of that?"

Livia watched as, with a killer grin, Joseph rolled his long, lean body to the side, retrieved something from the nightstand, and rolled back. When he came to his knees beside her, he held a very long, graduated vibe with a handle. Moving the toy to her lips, he ordered, "Lick."

Obediently, she touched the tip of her tongue to the toy, swirling it around the end. He hummed with approval.

"Although you're likely wet enough, the sight of this blue toy between your lips will help your king get a second wind." He changed the angle of the toy and murmured, "Suck," as he slid it into her mouth.

The taste of silicone was much less pleasant than the taste of Joseph, but she did her best to lubricate the large toy since she knew it was going into one of her nether places.

"That's my good girl," he praised before pulling it out. In her folded position, he didn't have to move to reach her pussy. Gentle fingers held her open, and he slid the slick head over her clit. It was more than enough to make her juices pool, although her wide-open, heels-over-head contortionist position had done a fine job with that, as did his ardent gaze devouring her so intimately.

Joseph changed the angle again and moved it back, dipping the tip into her center hole. He twirled it, making it extra wet then advanced it. The first two rings went in easily, but as he worked the ever-widening circles inside her, it became more challenging. By ring four, she tensed, her legs quivering in their restraints.

He looked up and captured her gaze.

"Color?"

"Green, Sire. But I don't know for how much longer."

Never losing their visual connection, he bent and licked her clit. Mesmerized by the sight of his lush mouth and agile tongue moving over her intimate flesh, she barely noticed as the large vibe sank in deeper.

After endless minutes of his sensual torment, he eased away, his eyes dipping to where he continued to play with the tapered toy. "I hadn't planned this tonight, but I can't resist having you this open for me." He withdrew the vibe from her pussy and moved it lower, gliding it over and around her smaller hole. "Your juices have you well prepared but tell me if it becomes too much and I'll add some lube."

The pressure was more than her muscles could resist, and the smallest circle slipped inside.

"Damn, blue and pink are my new favorite colors," he murmured, twisting the toy a bit as he advanced it to the next ring. "Let's add some spice."

Suddenly, the vibe came to life, its intensely powerful vibrations buzzing away in her naughtiest of places.

"Sire," she breathed, unable to put thoughts together to say much more.

With her head propped on a pillow, and her ass and pussy tilted toward the canopied top, she had a perfect view of what he was doing. Spread shockingly wide and left defenseless against whatever he wanted to do to her, she had no choice except to take what he gave her. Captive to his will, she didn't mind the least little bit.

As she watched, the third ring disappeared and worked unremittingly, slipping out to ring two then one, before pressing in again. She was really feeling the stretch and whimpered. Not from pain but reasonable apprehension over how many rings he planned to make her take. She'd counted six total, but anything past the halfway point would be unfamiliar territory.

His mouth lowered to her clit again, the circling and sucking of his clever tongue distracting her from the jumbo-sized toy a few inches below it. She felt his teeth and cried out at the same time ring four fully claimed her ass. Stretched to the limit, she became concerned he would go for a fifth.

"How are you doing, pet?"

A smart-ass remark about having the Michelin Man up her ass came to mind, but she bit it back.

Don't provoke the dom who controls the humongous toy, Olivia.

"It burns, master, and is really tight. I don't think I can take any more."

"Four is about what you'd get with me. King sized, if you will, and as much as I planned."

She blew out a relieved breath. "Thank you, Sire."

"You're very welcome, but thank me after I add this."

She got a glimpse of the metallic egg before he slipped it inside her. It didn't go far, his knowledgeable fingers pressing it right up against—

Her back bowed and her hips came off the bed, as much as the pillory would allow, as he switched it on. The vibrations against her G-spot took her instantly from needy to feverishly aroused, but that wasn't enough for him. Nope. The king wanted to play, keeping her on edge but not letting her soar off the cliff just yet.

When she neared climax, he eased off the egg, or reduced the pressure of his tongue. Sometimes he'd do both and turn on the vibe in her ass. Other times he'd pull back or pull it out—but never all the way—before reintroducing her to its graduated penetration.

There was so much going on between her legs, add to that the extreme position, the restraints and the clamps, double penetration plus Joseph wickedly tonguing her clit that she didn't know which sensation to focus on and found it impossible to absorb them all at once. After many long, exquisitely pleasurable minutes of stimulation overload she couldn't hold out any longer.

As if from a distance, she heard a panting, grunting moan. The roar in her ears as her climax built made it sound far off, but she knew it could only be her when the begging started.

Rolling her head on the pillows, she cried out, "Mercy, Sire. I can't take anymore."

"Then come, my queen, let me hear you scream your ruler's name."

Ultimately, the egg on her G-spot was to blame for her coming undone, occurring an instant after he thumbed the wicked oval on high. She bucked, her hips lifting higher off the bed. Her strained legs trembled, her torso twisting as she tried to escape her buzzing tormentors and the ceaseless lash of his wickedly hot tongue. Then, her mouth opened on a soundless wail.

The most intense orgasm in her life seemed to go on forever. After countless seconds, when it gradually abated, leaving a multitude of after-spasms in its wake, he had mercy and switched everything off.

The reprieve allowed her enough breath to utter raggedly, "Oh, my, freakin', king!"

Joseph chuckled. The rush of his heated breath on her over-sensitized pussy was nearly too much, producing helpless whimpers. He removed the egg and eased the tapered vibe from her ass. But he wasn't nearly through.

Kneeling between her thighs, he stroked his cock, ready to fill the void left by one of the toys.

"Where do you want me, pet?" he rasped, as he glided the head of his rampant erection along her slick, swollen lips.

"Inside me," she barely managed to say.

"Mmm. His Majesty's choice, then, as it should be."

In a blink, his considerable length was seated fully inside her pussy. Instead of fucking her hard, like she expected, he stilled, his hands moving to her breasts. "These need to come off, Livia. Ready?"

Even though it had been a while, the feeling was fresh in her mind. "Not really, Sire, but do it anyway."

Releasing the first clamp had her hissing, but Joseph's soothing tongue was there, quieting the unavoidable pain. The other went much the same way. He lingered, moving from one hard-tipped breast to the other, licking ever so gently.

"If only they didn't have to come off, hm?" Lifting his head, he gazed at her, clearly trying to gauge her readiness to continue.

"It's better now. Thank you."

With a kiss to each tender peak, he rose above her, nudging into her once more before he withdrew. His hands moved between her thighs and his thumbs spread her lips, slicking his wet cock back and forth over her clit. As she felt another stirring low in her belly, he moved lower. His girth, somewhere between ring three and four, filled her much tighter channel full, but with conscious effort and a shaky breath, she relaxed her bottom and let him sink in.

"That's my beautiful girl. Take what your master gives you."

He moved faster, soon pistoning in and out, using her tight ass as he would her pussy. She felt completely dominated by this, the ultimate of intimacies. After a few thrusts, with her overflowing pussy juices providing natural lube, she became consumed by his possession.

The stretch and fullness, enhanced by his constantly strumming thumb reawakening her clit, another orgasm started building.

A wave of ecstasy rolled inexorably toward her. Unable to hold back its force, she cried out, "I'm going to come again, Sire!"

"Come, my queen. By royal decree, I command it."

If she could have laughed, she would have. Instead, she screamed his name as euphoria crashed over her.

Whether the third, sixth, or one hundredth time, the pleasure he gave her was as gloriously fulfilling as the first. As she hung limply from the headboard, she watched as he experienced his own glory. With his head thrown back, his groan of pleasure became a husky growl in his throat as he came effusively inside her.

Olivia couldn't help but be moved by the enthralling sight.

Still slightly winded, he withdrew and quickly released her from the pillory. As limp as a dishrag, she couldn't have moved if she wanted to. Thank goodness for his strength and stamina. He rearranged the pillows then her, and followed a quick cleanup, with a deeply relaxing massage of her muscles and joints.

Afterward, they dozed while snuggled together, waking intermittently to share a kiss or a few soft words. Much later, Livia roused from the noises in the hallway—doors shutting, muffled voices, and laughter—clearly, it was closing time.

She stirred, whispering to Joseph, "It must be late. Shouldn't we go, too?"

"We don't have to leave just yet." He rolled her onto her back and came up on an elbow. His usually precise hair stuck out everywhere. She enjoyed seeing him mussed, especially when loving her was the cause, but brushed it off his forehead and finger combed it back into place.

"You're very handsome. Patrician, one might say. This room suits you."

He smiled, gazing down at her.

A thought occurred to her. "Can you see me without your Harry Potter glasses?"

He grunted, dropped onto his back, and dragged her on top. His hand went to her behind, which hadn't felt a single swat all night. She wiggled and pressed against him. His response was a firm squeeze.

"I'm nearsighted, pet. The answer is yes, but I'm usually likened to Harrison Ford in his Professor Jones days, not a boy wizard. I'll stick with that comparison, if you don't mind."

"I thought the same thing the first time I saw you. Professor Jones, it is." She grinned, her hand moving over his cheek and jaw, stroking the scruff of beard adorning both places. "I can easily see you in a teaching role, you know."

He smiled.

"What?"

"That's the room I tried to reserve for us tonight."

"A classroom?"

"Yes, I had visions of bending you over my desk and improving your grades."

"With a cane, no doubt."

"I'd thought to use a stout paddle." He sat up, toppling her from her perch. "That reminds me." He rolled and reached for something else on the nightstand. "You were such a good girl, I didn't get to use this."

He held up a paddle with *pet* emblazoned on one side and covered in red velvet on the other. She eyed it dubiously, imagining the word tattooed on her backside.

"That's too bad," she consoled in a sweet voice, although not one bit sorry. "Maybe next time."

"Nope. Now. Roll over."

"But, master, you said I was good."

"Since when do I need a reason to spank you?"

"Never," she grumbled, flipping onto her belly.

"Careful, or the few I intended will multiply." He patted her cheek. "Up on all fours, so I have a good target. I want to put my mark right on the fleshy part."

"Just what every girl wants to hear from her man, that she has a fleshy ass."

"I'm a dom, Livia. We like fleshy. It gives us so much more to discipline."

"Joseph..."

The paddle came down swiftly. "Have we ended the session, and I didn't know it?"

"No, sir."

"Better, but not quite right." He rubbed the velvety side where he had struck. "Care to try again?"

"No, the session hasn't ended, master."

"Very good." Leaning in, he inspected her paddled cheek. "Hm. That one didn't take. Lean back so your skin is nice and taut, as if I had you over a spanking bench with your knees cocked forward."

She adjusted her position.

"Perfect. Let's try that again." Unlike the cane and floggers he preferred, the paddle was silent as it soared through the air. The crack sounded before heat blossomed on her skin.

"Ouch!"

"Livia, I've bare-hand spanked you twice as hard as that and you didn't utter a word."

"This is different."

"How so?"

"Never mind."

Another splat fell on her other cheek. "I asked you a question, pet."

"It's different because you're not angry and I'm not—"

"What? Aroused? I can certainly fix that."

Two fingers slid into her wetness as his thumb found her clit. When the paddle fell again, he had it flipped to the padded side and gave her a half dozen whacks. By the time the sound from the last one abated, Livia was rocking back on his fingers, moaning softly.

"You're certainly aroused now, little one. You're dripping."

"It's your fingers, and when you spank me at the same time—" Abruptly, she stopped, as he added a third finger. After that, all that came out was an unintelligible groan.

"No coming yet, Livia. Not until we finish your tattoo."

The lettered side of the paddle fell hard on her unmarked cheek. She rocked back onto his hand, the pleasure-pain bringing her closer to the edge.

Whisper-soft, his fingers traced where he'd swatted. "Gorgeous. The word is as clear as can be. I'm going to see about ordering one of these for home." His lips brushed over her fiery skin, his breath hot as he whispered, "You may come now, pet."

His fingers drove quickly in and out as his tongue licked over the imprint on her cheek. In seconds, she was there, moaning as she experienced her fourth climax of the night.

Afterward, despite water and chocolate, she was hopelessly spent, her legs rubbery like overcooked noodles. So it was in the wee hours of the morning, Joseph, having swimmer's stamina, carried her upstairs to their borrowed apartment for the night.

Chapter 13

STANDING IMPATIENTLY outside Lifetime Fitness downtown, she checked her phone for the umpteenth time in the past ten minutes. He was late, and she wasn't about to go into the gym for the very first visit all alone. She sent him a quick message.

Livia: *Are you going to be too much longer? Should we reschedule the gym? Call me, please.*

Ten minutes later, she was pacing. Something must be wrong. Joseph was rarely late and when he was, he always called or at least sent her a text.

Livia: *Joseph, I'm worried. Please call.*

As soon as she hit send, she heard her name. Expecting to see him in yet another natty tweed suit, his long legs carrying him rapidly toward her, she turned with a welcoming smile. But it wasn't him striding toward her.

A coldness crept into her bones as she came face-to-face with the man she'd hoped to never see again. He was exiting the fitness center, his damp hair curling around his ears and at his neck, his handsome face wearing the all too familiar expression of superiority. He eyed her up and down slowly, and as he did so often in the past, frowned as if finding her lacking.

Livia's stomach clenched.

"Olivia, it's been a while."

"Vaughn." She barely stopped herself from calling him sir. He wasn't that to her anymore.

"Working out, eh? Good for you." His gaze dipped to the front of her formfitting racer-back tank then slid down to her roll-top, low-rise yoga pants. "Maybe if you had made the effort while we were together... But that's water under the bridge."

That stung. With an hourglass figure like her mother, she had curves and carried a little extra padding around her hips and thighs, but she wasn't fat. It had taken her a long time and many hours of therapy to realize that. But having him point it out made the old insecurities come rushing back.

In unforgiving spandex, she knew every bulge and ripple was conspicuous. Although she hated herself for doing so, she self-consciously moved her gym bag in front of her, hiding her hips.

Of course, he noticed. "Those stubborn ten pounds are still dogging you I see. Too bad, dearling. Without them, I might have kept you another year, maybe two."

His derisive words cut. She had to dig deep to maintain her composure. "I'd like to say it was nice to see you, Vaughn, but I prefer not to lie."

Managing an air of indifference, she shrugged coolly and turned away. That was the best she could do on the spur of the moment.

"Still bitter after all this time. That's sad. If you need help moving on, I have some older friends who might be interested."

She spun on him. "Are you for real?"

"Olivia, clearly you aren't over me. You're still angry."

"Of course, I'm angry. I devoted two years to you, and you cut me off at the knees, without warning. And where do you get off offering your 'older friends'? You're forty-six, Vaughn. That's not exactly a spring chicken."

A blonde stuck her head out the door behind him. "Mas—uh, Vaughn, sir. You forgot your wallet."

She tried to cover it, but Livia caught her slip. She also caught the puppy dog eyes she cast his way and felt nauseous. Had she acted like that?

The girl, and she was a girl, only twenty by her guess, was five feet eight and one hundred pounds at most. If she had breasts or hips, Livia couldn't tell.

"Thank you, Felicia." He accepted his wallet, pinched her chin between his thumb and finger—a hauntingly familiar gesture—then turned, summarily dismissing her.

The girl's smile slipped a bit as she went back inside.

"What happened to Allison?" Livia asked about the girl who'd come after her.

"Allison and I parted ways about a year ago. So, about those friends, John Stanton always found you attractive. I could—"

He really was a bastard. How had she been so blind?

"Didn't we attend John's fiftieth birthday party while we were together?"

"I believe we did. He is still a very vibrant man and active in the BDSM community."

That put him in his mid-fifties.

She stared at him for a moment, wondering at his power over women. "You realize that while she's buying her first legal drink, you'll be attending your thirtieth high school reunion?"

"Don't be petty, Olivia. Your number?"

"I'm seeing someone." She regretted telling him as soon as the words left her mouth.

"Are you now?" The inflection in his statement said he was doubtful. "Last I heard you were a club girl. I thought I taught you better than that." He patted his pockets as if searching for a pen. "Give me your number. I'll call you and you'll have mine when this guy fizzles out."

No. In fact, hell no!

That was what she wanted to say, but after years of intimidation, she didn't have the balls she needed to tell him that. So, she repeated coolly, "I have to go."

Done with the conversation, she moved away, but he grabbed her arm, swinging her back.

"Please, don't touch me."

"If it helps, you were my favorite."

Oh, my god! Did he really just say that?

Before her brain exploded, or she punched him like she really wanted to, she twisted her arm to get free. But he held fast.

"Let me go, Vaughn."

"So responsive, more than any submissive I've had before or since." He said this as if she hadn't spoken, but that didn't surprise her. He often ignored her, preferring to hear himself speak. "But time marches on for all of us," he continued, oblivious to her attempts to break free, "and things change."

"You know, I have one big regret."

Pretentious schmuck, as if he was God's gift to the submissives of this world, he said smugly, "You loved me, I know. And the way it ended, I—"

She finally snapped, her voice rising to near a shout. "No, you arrogant prick. My regret is ever having met you." She yanked her arm from his grasp, which had tightened painfully at her name-calling. "I rue that blackest of days. Do me a favor. If our paths ever cross again, have the courtesy to pretend we never met."

Proud of herself for not breaking down, she turned, and with an air of composure she didn't feel, walked to her car without looking back.

Once inside, she glanced in her rearview mirror and saw him looking after her. From this distance, she could see his anger, evident by the ruddiness of his cheeks. That she'd rattled him with the ugly scene gave her a small sense of satisfaction. With nervous fingers, she started her car and steered it toward home, seeing a large glass of alcohol in her imminent future.

Fifteen minutes later, she was pulling into Joseph's drive when her phone rang. With a brief glance at the screen, she saw it was him and promptly ignored the call. If he knew, he'd be incensed. But she wasn't calm enough to talk to him yet.

After a glass of wine, maybe two, she might be up to it, but not now. Her voice mail alert sounded as she pulled into the garage. A text soon followed.

Joseph: *I'm at the gym and you are not. Court went very late and my phone died. My apologies, pet, but I'm glad you didn't wait. I'm going to swim my laps and will be home directly after.*

In a few minutes, after pouring the largest wineglass she could find full to the brim with a sweet red, she sent her reply.

Livia: *Sounds like a stressful day. Enjoy your swim. I have a headache and am going straight to bed. See you in the morning.*

She ended it with a heart emoji as always. After a large mouthful of wine, she topped off her glass, carrying it along with the rest of the bottle to the master bath to fill the Jacuzzi tub.

A WARM BODY AGAINST her back, the gentle glide of a hand over the curve of her hip, and the prickle of sunlight against her eyelids pulled her from sleep. Livia arched into a long morning stretch, but the shooting pain in her head cut it short. Her hand flew to her forehead as she groaned.

"Did you drink the entire bottle?" His voice was gruff from sleep and not overly loud, but it was enough to hurt her alcohol-abused brain.

"No." She whispered the denial.

"Livia," he replied in a skeptical tone. "The empty bottle was on the counter."

"The last bit I poured down the sink to prevent having another glass in a moment of inebriated weakness."

"Because I was late? I'm sorry for that, but surely you understand—"

"No." She twisted to face him. "When you were late, I was worried that something was wrong, but that wasn't it. I had a terrible day." Livia pressed her pounding forehead against his chest. "Today isn't starting out so great, either."

"A wine hangover is worse than anything. I'll get you some aspirin and water." He twisted to roll out of bed.

"Wait. Hold me a minute first?"

She knew she sounded pathetic but having his arms around her would go further than aspirin ever could. As his long arms enveloped her, she let slip a ragged sigh.

"Tell me what happened."

His order rumbled in his chest beneath her ear. She'd do anything to avoid talking about it and snuggled deeper into him, nuzzling against the warm, smooth skin beneath her cheek.

"No stalling," he warned. Then, too damn perceptive for her own good, he added, "Remember our discussion about secrets and lies of omission."

Burying her face in his neck, her voice came out muffled. "I ran into Vaughn at the fitness center."

He stiffened. "I thought he was teaching in Chicago."

"So did I, but apparently, he's back. I'd like to think the co-eds at Northwestern sent him packing. They must have more intelligence than those at UT. He was with a new one who didn't look old enough to drink yet."

"He upset you enough to down a bottle of wine. Do you still have feelings for him, Livia?"

"Yes, anger, disgust, loathing." She propped her forearm on his chest and looked down at him. "No good feelings, Joseph, I swear. Mostly I'm angry at myself for falling for such a prick—excuse my French—and throwing two years of my life away."

"What did he say to you?"

"The usual demeaning remarks."

"He got to you." His arms tightened.

Her hand rose to push back her tangled mass of hair. Suddenly, he caught her wrist, stretching out her arm. "What the fuck! He put his hands on you?"

She followed his eyes to the ring of bruises around her upper arm. Four finger marks and a thumbprint were clearly visible. Her fingers came up to probe the discolored skin gently, hissing at an especially tender spot.

"I'm gonna kill the bastard."

"No, you're not," she replied firmly. "Although I appreciate the bloodthirstiness on my behalf, he's a jerk from my past and you can't kill them all." Her hand rose to his cheek. "I met a lot of jerks before I met you, Joseph. Thank you for breaking the streak."

"I hate I wasn't there to protect you." His tone took on a scary rasp when he added, "And to beat him to a bloody pulp."

"I got in a few good licks. They were verbal, but I was proud of myself."

"You stood up to him?"

"Even better, I hit him where it hurts. I called him old."

"I'm still going to kill him."

She swung her leg over his middle and straddled him. With both hands framing his face, she insisted, "He isn't worth it."

His hands curled around her hips. "He might not be, but you are."

That was so sweet. Livia fell in love with him even more.

"You can't kill the worm. Who'd hold me if you're on death row for murder? This is Texas, you know. That's a hangin' offense in these parts."

Her attempt at lightening the mood fell flat as his eyes searched her face intently. Finally, he nodded. "Because you asked, I won't kill the bastard. I'll ruin him instead."

Chapter 14

AFTER THE INCIDENT, Joseph fumed for days. He blamed himself for not being on time and considered it a personal failure that he wasn't there to defend her. Livia knew it haunted him. Each time he saw the bruises on her arm, he planted tender kisses on the discolored skin. They had faded by the following weekend, along with most of Joseph's anger. He no longer brooded over the disturbing event, but she could tell he hadn't forgotten, becoming more protective and almost hypervigilant with her safety.

Another week passed. Although Livia wanted to switch gyms or not go at all, Joseph coaxed her back. He accompanied her each time, ever watchful. She suspected he was hoping to run into Vaughn, but much to her relief, they didn't.

By the end of the workweek, they were ready to unwind and headed back to San Antonio. Emma and David's guest visit was approved, so they joined them. Since it was Friday, and Elena's night off, the lounge and bar were busy but not bursting at the seams as on her prior visits. It was a different story when they entered the jam-packed playroom where it looked like all two hundred members had come out to play.

Although she was still new herself, and she hadn't seen all there was to see, she enjoyed watching her friends' initial reaction to the Decadence dungeon. Awestruck, Emma's jaw seemed perpetually unhinged, her mouth open as she blatantly stared, and David's eyes darted around the room, trying to take everything in at once.

"Did I look like that?" she whispered to Joseph.

He glanced at their guests and smiled indulgently. "I think everyone does when they get their first look."

It was little wonder. Livia wasn't used to it herself. Everywhere she looked, couples, and occasionally small groups, were engaged in some sort of kinky play. The smell of sex and leather permeated the air. And the discordant sounds of erotic play—groans of passion, cries of erotic pain, and the rhythmic *thwacks* and *thuds* of floggers and paddles—combined to produce a unique sort of music.

Like her last visit, a couple performed under the spotlight on the elevated stage. This time, wooden stocks restrained the male submissive. His domme, a voluptuous platinum blonde in red leather, vigorously pumped her hips and rode him hard with a strap-on from behind. Every few strokes, she brought down her leather strap with a resounding crack across his already red buttocks. Each lash made Livia wince, but from his hoarse cries of, "More, please, mistress," he apparently enjoyed.

Still stunned by the blatant sex on display, Livia turned to see David and Emma's response. Both stood bugged-eyed and slack-jawed in shock. She tugged on Joseph's hand to get his attention.

When he saw their stupefied expressions, he chuckled. "Did I mention our private dungeon has no restrictions on sex or bare genitals like the public clubs do?"

"Uh, no," David replied, his lips turning up in a rapt grin. "I think I would have remembered that part."

"Holy cow," Emma murmured, trying to recover, but her mouth still stood agape. "David, uh, sir," she breathed. "If we can't get a private room for tonight, I might need to visit the bar first."

Livia giggled. "No worries. Joseph has you covered. He reserved the Sultan's Chamber for you." She took her finger and lifted Emma's chin, but immediately felt open again. "It's the most popular theme room. I've never been, but I've heard all about it. You're gonna love it."

"Your reservation is in half an hour," Joseph added, "so there's only time for the nickel tour."

Walking the circuit, he pointed out the less common pieces of bondage equipment as they made their way to the stairs at the back of the room. After Joseph introduced them to the DM controlling access to the upper level, they parted ways. David leading a giddy Emma upstairs, while Joseph guided Livia to the station he had reserved.

It wasn't long before he had her stripped and bound to a St. Andrew's Cross. Instead of facing the eight-foot-tall wooden X, he had restrained her with her back to it, facing the onlookers standing three deep around the station. The only thing that protected her modesty was the minuscule G-string he had provided with her black, sparkly, super-short sheath dress. Livia had no doubt that very soon, they, too, would be history.

As she looked out at the crowd beyond the red velvet ropes, she noted many were younger, thinner, and by her discerning eye, more beautiful. Vaughn's recent comments about her body and how her excess weight contributed to him dumping her,

both long-held self-doubts, clung to her consciousness. Like
scars on her soul, they crept to the surface and her anxieties
grew.

Reflexively, she pulled at her wrist cuffs, which held firm.
Joseph rose from a crouch, where he had been buckling a cuff
around her ankle. His observant gaze scanned her face, and he
astutely identified her unease. In shirtsleeves and dark trousers,
his sport coat and tie discarded for their session, he moved in
close. His long hard frame covering the entirety of her much
shorter one, hiding her from the curious eyes of the spectators.
One hand curled around her hip while the other curled around
her nape, his long fingers threading through her hair.

"You're on edge, little one. A certain amount of apprehension is expected, but you're working yourself into a panic. Slow
your breathing."

"Can't we get a room upstairs, master?"

"No, they're all booked tonight, and we gave ours to David
and Emma. Focus on calming your mind, pet."

"I'm trying."

"Keep your eyes on me, Livia."

She looked up, doing as he ordered, but movement behind
him had her gaze drifting back to the crowd that had grown
and now stood four or five deep on the other side of the ropes.

His fingers in her hair tightened, and the heel of his hand
on her jaw turned her face back to his. "What's this really
about?"

Her lashes lowered, not wanting to disappoint him. She
shook her head. "It's nothing. I'm fine."

"Are you sure you want to go with that?" he challenged,
knowing full well it was a lie.

"No."

"What's the truth, baby? It's something because you're trembling."

She grimaced. He was too darn perceptive. It was like being with a mind reader.

"Look at me."

When her lashes swept up, his face was so close she could see the tiny flecks of gold and brown scattered throughout the green of his irises. As he spoke, his minty breath brushed her mouth, his lips a mere whisper away. Passion filled his words as he spoke with searing intensity.

"You're gorgeous, every square inch of you inside and out. So much so, I want to show you off. I want the members, both new and long-since jaded, to witness the beauty of your submission. It's in the swelling of your breasts at the sound of my voice, the quiver in your belly as you anticipate my touch, and when you come, the rapturous expression on your face is nothing short of breathtaking. That's something to revel in. I'm not a full-bore exhibitionist, but I'd like to share the beauty of my submissive occasionally. Can you give me that, pet?"

She sought the truth of his words and found it shining in his eyes as steadfast and clear as the brightest star in the sky. That he believed she was beautiful was all that mattered to her.

"You've given me so much. I want to give you that in return, master."

"And I'm honored by the gift." Whisper soft, his lips touched hers. "Would a blindfold help?"

"I think it might."

"I have one in my bag." Another kiss followed, much too brief but filled with passion. "Be right back."

He stepped away, bending to his bag on the floor. While she waited, she closed her eyes, blocking out the avid voyeurs and focusing only on what Joseph planned next.

"Gorgeous, albeit a little hefty and long in the tooth."

Gasps from the crowd followed the outrageously rude comment. Her eyes flew wide. Immediately, she found the speaker in the crowd. His face twisted into a derisive sneer; Vaughn stood only four feet away.

Feelings of inadequacy rushed over her in a torrent of self-doubt. She jerked at her bindings, wanting only to cover herself and hide from his judgements and spiteful criticisms. Over-whelming panic set in and she did the only thing she could think of.

"Red! Joseph. Red!"

In less than a second, he was beside her. "I'm here, pet. You're safe."

His reassuring voice and his hand at her waist eased her to a certain degree, but not enough. She wanted Vaughn gone, or to be gone herself.

She felt his eyes on her briefly, then he turned, searching the crowd. The members were all staring at her ex-dom, giving him censorious glares. They also stepped back, giving him a wide berth, so it wasn't rocket science to figure out who had spoken.

"That's Steros, isn't it?" Joseph confirmed needlessly, his voice shaking with barely contained rage.

"Can we go somewhere else, master?"

"What did he do, Livia?"

"He said some most unkind things, Master J," a familiar, feminine voice stated. It was Mara, standing at the ropes. "I'll stay with her if you'd like to deal with that pig."

"Get her down, Mara. This won't take long."

What happened next was a sight to see. Joseph hurdled the velvet ropes and, in a flash, had Vaughn by the throat. Having at least six inches in height on the worm, and with far superior strength, his fists in his collar lifted him off the floor then slammed him against the nearest wall.

"What's this about?" Master Sean demanded, seeming to materialize out of nowhere. At his back was Megan's husband, Tony. Both wore DM badges on a band around their arms.

"This piece of shit had the gall to talk to my sub while in a scene. He insulted her. He's also the son of a bitch who abused her. I want him out—permanently."

"You can't do that," Vaugh whined, wheezing when Joseph's fists tightened. "I merely made an observation."

"Not true," someone in the crowd called out. "He was deliberately rude."

"He insulted her," said another, "in a most insolent tone and manner."

"I heard it all." This came from a woman who Livia recognized as the domme from the scene on center stage earlier. Her sub, who towered above his diminutive mistress, was standing protectively in front of her as if ready to do battle. She had a small hand on his biceps, stroking him in a calming manner. "It's appalling, really, that any dom at Club Decadence would treat another's sub so disrespectfully. I second Master Joseph's motion. He needs to go, and not return."

"Demeaning submissives isn't something we tolerate," Tony said with authority. "Unless you're implying that it was part of a planned scene. Were you invited to play out a humiliation session, by chance?"

"No," he snapped. "As if—"

Whatever he intended to say was cut off by Joseph's hands twisting his collar.

"He's turning blue, Joe," Sean stated quietly.

When he eased the tension, Vaughn sucked in a breath and choked, "Who are you to throw me out? Where is Master Dex?"

"These are two of the owners, and Mistress Anne is a charter member, you pathetic putz." Joseph's rage hadn't diminished and his voice, usually a soothing melodic tenor, had lowered to a harsh growl. "Not to mention this is a private club and they can throw out whoever they damn well please."

"I'm a renowned author with a PhD! They won't choose me over a chubby secretary. I want to see Master Dex."

Joseph's fist connecting with Vaughn's middle-aged paunch cut off his grating whine. A sickening crunch sounded next when he followed it with a punch in the face. After that, he released his hold, letting Vaughn drop to the floor with a loud thud, blood spurting from his nose.

He groaned initially before squealing like the pig Mara had likened him to. "You broke my nose! I'll sue."

"Excellent," Joseph snarled. "We can bring to light how you prey on innocent young women from your classes, abuse your authority, subjugate them, and crush their spirit. I relish the day I have you in a courtroom."

Mistress Anne murmured, "Obviously this rube doesn't know he's dealing with the finest criminal attorney in the state."

"Try to find a job after that goes public," Sean sneered.

"Or a club to play in," Cap added.

"Already taken care of," Joseph put in.

"You!" the bleeding worm accused. "It was you who had me blackballed. They canceled my membership at the gym, too."

"I've only just begun. I have an appointment with the dean of your department on Monday at ten o'clock sharp."

"Your firm donates generously to UT Austin, don't they, Joe?"

"Indeed, Sean. It is five out of six of our partners' alma mater, mine included." He looked down at Vaughn coldly as he launched his last salvo. "You don't have tenure yet, do you? What a shame."

"You can't. I'll be ruined," came his wheedling whine.

Joseph shrugged, a smirk on his face as he fixed his sleeves, obviously delighted by the idea of Vaughn's career going down the toilet.

A soft blanket falling across her shoulders alerted Livia that she was free of the cross. So wrapped up in the drama playing out before her, she'd barely registered anything else. She looked up into Master Dex's midnight-blue eyes.

"Are you all right, little one?"

"Yes, sir. Just shook up a bit."

"I'm sorry this happened, Olivia. We'll make sure he won't bother you again."

"Thank you." Her worried gaze returned to where Joseph still loomed over Vaughn. "Do you think you can intervene, Master Dex, and make sure Joseph doesn't kill him?"

"I'm on my way to do just that, but I can't say I'd be doing the club or the world as a whole any favors. The man's a horse's ass."

After giving Livia's shoulder a squeeze, Dex moved to Joseph's side and weighed in. "You're no longer welcome at Decadence, Steros, and will be blackballed statewide after I make some calls."

"This is ludicrous. I demand a vote."

Anger emanated off Dex in waves. "Fine. Luckily, Joseph, Anne, Sean, and Cap are all on the membership committee. All in favor of dismissal?"

Four "ayes" rang out in the eerily silent room.

"And my vote makes five, which is a quorum and all it takes, you miserable fuck." Turning away in disgust, Dex looked to Sean and Cap. "If you two don't mind taking out the trash, it's beginning to stink."

Titters of laughter sounded from the audience now that the owners had the ugly scene well in hand, not that Joseph needed any help. He stood silently watching until the two big owners/DMs hauled him up by the arms and escorted him none-too-gently to the exit. Only then did Joseph turn and return to her side.

"Your taste in doms certainly has improved, honey," Mara said with a wink as she relinquished her hold on Livia's shoulders. Since her dom had arrived and was providing her protection, she slipped back on the other side of the ropes.

Ignoring the applause and *atta boys* that ensued, Joseph scooped her up and carried her to a nearby couch. As he sat with her cuddled in his lap, she could feel his body vibrating, his anger far from appeased. Her hand rose to his cheek.

"He's gone. It's over."

"Not until he's across the border in some other state." He glanced down at her. "But you let me worry about that, pet. Are you all right?"

"Shaken a bit, but watching you go all kick-ass alpha on his butt made me feel a lot better."

He buried his face in her hair, hugging her close. A moment later, his lips nuzzled along her throat and he murmured huskily, "While I had my hands around his throat, I wanted to choke the life out of him."

"I figured as much, but I'm glad you didn't."

"I know. You don't think he's worth it."

"That and because Texas doesn't allow conjugal visits."

It started out low, only a small tickle against her skin, but it quickly became a rumble of his laughter in his chest.

She squirmed on his lap until she faced him, her breasts against his chest and could wind her arms around his neck. Against his ear, she whispered, "Now that his nonsense is over, can we resume our session?"

His head came up. "You want to continue after that?"

"We came all this way to play and barely got started. Not to mention, David and Emma are enjoying the room we had reserved for ourselves for weeks in advance. Don't let him spoil our evening. Please?"

"You're sure? That was quite a scare, and you were nervous before that."

"It's like falling off the wagon, isn't it? You gotta dust your-self off and get right back on, right?"

That got her a small smile. "You're mixing your idioms, pet. I believe you mean a horse."

"A wagon, a horse, or a cross." She shrugged, grinning up at him. "I'm game for anything as long as it's with you, master."

Her smile was infectious, and he returned it fully.

"You are so precious to me. I love you, Livia."

"I love you, too, Joseph." Her lips brushing his as she spoke incited him to swoop in for a heated kiss. When he released her, she blinked while sorting out her head enough to make sense. "Please say you'll do whatever kinky stuff you had planned for me. Seeing you beat he-who-from-now-on-shall-remain-nameless's ass made me wet."

A full-throated laugh was his answer as he rose and carried her back to the cross.

THE BRUSHED LEATHER tails of his lash fell across her breasts, sending a jolt of pleasure shooting straight to her clit. She writhed in her cuffs, her back bowing off the cross. A teas-ing lick stroked her belly, the next striking in an upswing be-tween her spread legs.

"Master, please," she gasped, not sure how much more she could take.

"Come, Livia. Show them how beautiful you are when you fly apart for me."

The flogger didn't stop, brushing her thighs, her ribs, the underside of each breast then, once more, landing a direct hit on her pussy. Her head strained backward as much as the cross would allow and her mouth fell open on a guttural cry of ecstasy. Her body hummed with her release as she felt Joseph move against her, his lips brushing her throat, her shoulders, each nipple then his hardness surged inside her.

His thick cock filling her extended the delicious shivers of her climax. As he drove into her, what had begun to ebb resurged. The tightness low in her belly spread upward, rising to her swollen breasts and forward to her still tingling clit.

"I'm going to come again."

"Do it, pet," he groaned in her ear. "Squeeze me hard when you come, and I'll be right there with you."

IT WAS JUST PAST MIDNIGHT. Joseph and Livia were cozied up on a comfy love seat in the lounge chatting quietly with Sean and Mara, Tony and Megan, and Dex and Elena. They were all enjoying an after-session drink, mostly nonalcoholic, when David and Emma exited the playroom. Both had identical sated smiles on their faces. David was exerting considerable effort keeping a jelly-legged Em on her feet. Cap hauled his petite wife into his lap to make room on the couch for them.

Livia grinned at her friends. "What did you think of the Sultan's chamber?"

"Words cannot express..." Em sighed. "This place is a kink-inclined, power exchange couple's dream come true. I guarantee no one had a more eventful night than Sultan David and his naughty concubine."

Livia glanced at Mara who shared a look with Elena and Megan. As one, they erupted into giggles, their doms joining in with chuckles and amused grins.

Em looked at David. "Did I say something funny?"

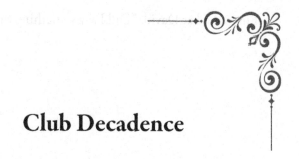

Club Decadence

the sensual thrill ride continues...

FAITHFULLY: A CLUB Decadence Novella, Book 3.5

In the summer of 1979, single, smart, college-bound Joanna Beckett has her eye on the future. She isn't looking for love, but when she runs into Captain Peter Davis, who is nearly ten years her senior, she is smitten and falls for his warm heart, sharp mind, and commanding embrace.

Despite his commitment to his career, Peter can't resist funny, flirtatious, sexy Joanna. Although she's too young and occasionally too sassy for her own good, she's an Army brat and knows separations are part of the deal. After a whirlwind romance, he makes Joanna his blushing bride.

As this duo navigates the highs and lows of building a life together, their very special love leads to the founding of Club Decadence. But can this thirty-plus-year marriage survive Peter's desire to un-retire from the service just as Joanna finally gets the chance to be the only priority in his life?

Publisher's Note: *Faithfully* is a prequel to the Club Decadence series. It was originally included in the *Hearts Ablaze* Valentines anthology which is no longer available. It is novella length and has been revised, reedited, and re-covered. All the books in the series are steamy, suspense-filled romances that contain power exchange and BDSM, which may be disturbing to some.

Other Titles by
Maddie Taylor

DEVIL'S PLAYGROUND: DARK REFUGE BOOK 1

In the wake of her father's murder, Carina fled her life of luxury. She manages to stay one step ahead of her deranged, duplicitous uncle and Nick Devlin, the gorgeous FBI agent who stole her heart then crushed it. As she struggles to survive and stay out of sight, she soon realizes Nick is her only hope of coming out of her predicament alive.

Nick has been searching for the right woman for a very long time. When Carina turns to him for protection, she succumbs to his devilish charm once again. As his dark side unleashes her wicked desires, he knows deep down that his search is over. All that remains is keeping her safe from the Mob and winning back her trust for good.

Just as Carina starts to believe a new life with Nick is possible, her deadly past and a vengeful Godfather resurface with a chilling demand. There can be no peace, and he won't rest until more of the family's blood is spilled.

Publisher's Note: *Devil's Playground* is an extra-long, stand-alone romance in the Dark Refuge series. It contains a hot FBI agent with a protective streak a mile wide. When he gives an official order, he expects to be obeyed. The same as when he plays. If such material offends you, do not buy this book.

THE BARBARIAN'S CAPTIVE

(Primarian Mates, Book 1)

Light years from home, plant biologist Lt. Eva La Croix and her all-female exploration team land on a planet they believe is a perfect substitute for the dying Earth. They are set upon by huge alien hunters, and Eva is captured by the barbarian leader. Tossed over his shoulder, she is carried back to camp and claimed as his own.

Despite her fear, she is captivated by the gorgeous, dominant male with his long, gleaming black hair, smooth bronze skin, and glimmering golden eyes. Expecting her full compliance, he strips her and prepares her for an intimate and very thorough inspection. Horrified, Eva protests, but quickly learns defiance will be met with swift consequences, including a bare-bottom spanking until he proves to her who is in command.

Deemed compatible, she and her teammates are whisked away to the barbarians' world where they are mated to these powerful men. While pampered and protected, the women are expected to submit to their males' authority and bear their young. Will Eva learn to adapt to their unusual beliefs and old-fashioned ways? Can she sacrifice her independence and surrender to this dynamic, highly sexual alien male who has conquered her body, and perhaps her heart? Or when escape is imminent, will she flee with the others, never to see him again and feel the rampant desire that now surges through her blood for her compelling barbarian mate?

MARSHAL'S LAW
(Jackson Brothers series, Book 1 of 3)

When Janelle Prescott is thrown from her car as it careens off a slippery road, she expects to wake up in a hospital. Instead, to her utter disbelief, she wakes up in a jail cell which looks like something from an old western movie set. It is there, hurt and alone, with no idea what happened or how she will get back home, that Janelle first meets Aaron Jackson. As she regains her wits, however, Janelle realizes that something is terribly amiss, and her worst fears are confirmed when she learns that Aaron is the marshal of Cheyenne County, Wyoming...and the year is 1878.

When an injured, apparently addle-headed woman falls into his lap, Aaron takes it upon himself to keep her safe and nurse her back to health. Truth be told, he is instantly attracted to her despite her sharp tongue and her bizarre story—a story which the evidence quickly forces him to accept as genuine. After Aaron takes her under his wing and into his family's home, the two clash frequently, but Aaron is more than ready to lay down the law...even if that means a good, hard, bare-bottom spanking for this feisty brat from another era.

Having little choice, Janelle must learn how to live as a woman in the Old West, including submitting to the firm-handed marshal who, in spite of everything, seems to have laid claim to her heart.

TOUGH LOVE: MANDY'S TAKE-CHARGE DADDY

Between work and play, life is pretty intense for them both. As Aiden introduces Amanda to his brand of loving, things promise to get even hotter.

Except when Aiden senses his bride is holding back, he'll stop at nothing, even resorting to tough love to earn her complete trust. Can a special weekend with Aiden convince Mandy to take a chance on her groom who is also her forever love?

TOUGH LOVE 2: DADDY'S GOLDEN RULES

Krista Evans knows exactly how cruel life can be. When she was twelve, she lost her dad to war. Then her mother disappeared into the bottom of a bottle. Her heart has been broken, her money stolen, and she's had more than one run-in with the law. What the girl needs is a break. She just can't seem to catch one.

Sheriff Samuel Golden is a lonely man with nothing but work to fill his time. When he busts a pretty young blonde in the midst of a theft, he's tempted by his immediate attraction to her. She's guilty as sin despite her protests to the contrary, but Sam can sense there's a lost little girl inside of her who just needs to be taught right from wrong.

In lieu of jail, Sam agrees to take Krista in hand for thirty days for some bare-bottom rehabilitation. But when their obvious chemistry becomes unavoidable, Sam will have to choose: resist the lure of the girl who so desperately needs a stern-yet-loving daddy, or banish the ghosts of his past.

TOUGH LOVE 3: DISAPPOINTING HER DADDIES

Erica has been working for D&G Construction for five years. Coincidentally, that's how long she's been hopelessly in love with Daniel and Grayson, the two gorgeous men who work down the hall from her who also happen to sign her paycheck. Neither sees her as anything more than the naive college girl they first hired. The fact she has no issue being shared by both of these dominant daddies, and boldly tells them so, finally opens their eyes to the perfect submissive who's been right in front of them all along.

Things are going well for them, both at work and at play, when Erica makes a costly mistake on an important contract. She must confess and face the consequences. Most employees would be fired on the spot, but Dan and Gray are more inclined to take their naughty girl over their knees for a bare-bottom lesson she won't soon forget. Fortunately, their unconditional love for her, combined with an eleventh-hour solution to save the company, means her daddies can make it all better in much more pleasurable ways.

TOUGH LOVE 4: SLOW BURN DADDY

As a little girl, Piper Monroe didn't have the luxury of believing in fairy tales. Abandoned by her father and left with her alcoholic mother, she and her three siblings grew up fast. Years later, when Lieutenant Brody Murphy of Boston Fire rescues Piper from a burning building, the handsome-as-sin firefighter does more than just save her life. He shows her kindness, gives her a place to stay, and makes her question everything she thought she knew about knights in shining armor.

Nurturing and tender, Brody is happy to be patient with Piper as she struggles to accept his feelings and her own desires. But he won't let her tightly built walls stand between them forever. Proving to her that he's the type of man who won't bail when life gets difficult is just the beginning. Will Piper's heart finally open up to the tough but unconditional slow-burn love she's always needed?

Follow Maddie
Online

Scan the QR code for all Maddie's Links

<u>Get a FREE Maddie Taylor Romance!</u>
Keep up with author news, get new release updates and cover reveals before anyone else, as well as sneak previews, and lots of giveaways.
Subscribe to Maddie's newsletter ⇨ scan <u>the QR code for the subscribe link</u>

Made in the USA
Monee, IL
08 December 2024

72741620R00115